For those who believed
And would not forgive me
Until I started to.

The Haircut: Stories & Fragments

A ShoppedAround Book published in agreement with Wonderland Games, Inc.

Publishing History: Wonderland Games Edition, December 2016

Published in the United States of America

1 3 5 7 9 10 8 6 4 2

ISBN 9780692844434

Cover art and book design by Angelo Rosales.

The Haircut

Stories & Fragments

Dana Gorbea-Leon

The house was quiet and the world was calm.
The reader became the book; and summer night

Was like the conscious being of the book.
The house was quiet and the world was calm.

The words were spoken as if there was no book,
Except that the reader leaned above the page,

Wanted to lean, wanted much to be
The scholar to whom his book is true, to whom

The summer night is like a perfection of thought.
The house was quiet because it had to be.

The House was Quiet and the World was Calm
Wallace Stephens

There are at least two kinds of Games.
One could be called finite, the other infinite.
A finite game is played for the purpose of winning,
an infinite game for the purpose of continuing to play. ...

Finite and Infinite Games
James P. Carse

Contents

Stories & Fragments

Gypsies

I live in what some call the bastard end of the city, past where its easternmost edge languishes and unincorporated stretches of third-rate homes, lumpish apartment buildings and pain-filled businesses (bargain basements, clearance emporiums, impound lots, money-transfer mills, loan brokers, storefront houses of worship, discard bays, segundas) squat cheek-by-jowl on some point of the compass the rest of the city believes barely exists. There are hills here, the occasional tree shade to squatters and gypsies. But I exaggerate. The closest thing to gypsy wagons are the incessant parade of shopping carts you skirt or outrun to get from one side of the street to the other. The men and women attached to the carts stoop, ever on guard of their possessions, which, don't let anyone fool you, must be quite substantial despite appearances, the piles of derelict excess like the hillsides, mud-covered and hulking and strangely graceful, the juddering cartwheels build on some model that long ago anticipated the weight. Blasted territory, the end of the murmur of things divine and the beginning of homeless passions. (I don't think the street-corner evangelist was quoting scripture.)

1

I live here in a one-room walkup because the rent is low, you're allowed to skip a month's rent now and then — someone would have to put up a sign, someone would have to interview prospects, someone would have to make a choice they might live to regret — and people don't bother you unless you bother them. Most days in fact, everyone's quite friendly, especially the squatters.

"Yo! You gonna eat that?"

"Brotha, brotha, brotha. When youse dun wit' that can I has it? I believes I can still read."

"Man, somebodys dun'ah numbah onya cuz youse looks like'ya momma's done died."

"¿Oye, tú mama sabe que tú eres un maricón?"

That doesn't sound quite right, but I take it on like any other compliment, for what else could it be? Right now, mid-morning, winter light strikes a dazzling note on a scene otherwise absent of color. No one here can afford a new winter coat, a daub of paint on chipped windows or doors, the energy to barter for bargains at this year's super sales. But listen to how everyday conversation turns to reminiscence. Things are bound to get better, have to get better, if only we remember who we are, where we've been. Memory is the only dogma here, the only strategy, the only advance.

The voice on the phone sounds anxious. "M'ijo, it says," (she still calls me that), "m'ijo, I just want to make sure you're all right."

"Mom, someone's at the door."

"Is it the landlord again?"

"How would I know, I haven't answered it yet? Mom, I have to go."

2

Somehow, someone's always at the door, the shower's running, the toaster's popping up, when she calls. She speaks to a part of me I'd rather not give into. I am waiting for someone to call about an interview, the prospect, the possibility, the pretense, and I'd like to be on my best behavior. According to the news the economy's turning around; it's bound to elbow its way here, eventually. Here: in, or at, the place where you are, or at a place near you. Here: used to draw attention to a particular point or stage in a situation. Here: used to indicate that an event or situation is, tiresomely or irritatingly, about to repeat itself: here we go again. Here, where one week from now they'll find my body, slumped across the kitchen counter, bullet to the back of the head, gangland style.

But that was just a dream (or a going concern), like the gypsies. Soon to fade, like the gypsies, when it's time to fold up tents and pack up wagons and head North or South or East or West, on some impossible trek, some impossible fancy, somewhere out there, beyond the horizon, on the fictitious mean on the hour's angle.

The Drawer

Looking into the camera, dead-on, almost smiling, almost posed, almost relaxed, back when my hair was still black. To say he's been waiting for this moment, when I'd be ransacking the drawer, looking for something I'd inevitably lost, to find me, staring back across, what, 30 years, that I was young once, that I had promise once, that that smile means he knew, somehow, it has yet to be fulfilled, would be to say too much. I still have the tie somewhere in my closet; the shirt? the color has come back in season, if not the style. The shoulders are my shoulders but the hands belong to someone else, less attached — *he* could afford to give up what he didn't have, didn't think of having, didn't yet want to have, the tide would turn, he'd push past the moment, something would turn up.

∞

Hair cropped military style, Nathan at my side. He's taller than I remember, and I'm happier than I recall. My whole face is smiling, chin bone to brow line, the ears tipped back in surprise, didn't hear the punch line coming, and yes it was a hoot. Did we dress to match? The sun is in front of us and our shadows thrown rearward cross. Someone from a different century,

Northern latitudes, a brooding cast of mind, would have made a fairytale of that. He's in Florida now, or Tennessee, Jacksonville, Orlando, Gatlinburg, Pigeon Forge, the continental divide not deep or wide enough, distance and time, distance and time.

∞

Waikiki Beach, Honolulu, Hawaii, 1982. Dark as a coconut and buffed up to attract. Anthony, Roscoe, Vance. Snorkeling, hula-dancing, poi, everyone smiling, because, well, we're in paradise. Once or twice in those ten days, I fell in love and almost meant it. They did too I suppose. I changed the sheets twice a day, everyday. Suntan oil and sea spray and god-knows what else. The days and nights were never long enough. Anthony had a Brooklyn accent, Roscoe hazel eyes, Vance a laugh that dipped and rose in all the wrong places until sometime after midnight he'd tamed it with rum. I slept through most of the plane ride there, and the entire plane ride back.

∞

There's no picture of the bride and groom. If there is, it's gone missing. Just my sister and me, in all our finery, bride and best man. Her idea. Las Vegas wedding, drive-thru chapel, rented priest. Quickie marriage, quickie divorce. Her fourth and his second. I have to say I look quite handsome, single-breasted suit, waistcoat shading to plum. My contact lenses phase. A rather wry (rueful?) look in the eyes — did I know what was coming? did she know I knew? Her fourth and his second. You would have thought they'd have settled into what they wanted by then. Hair parted left to right. Should try that again. My neck looks thicker, somewhat constrained. I don't remember feeling strapped in, by suit or by circumstance. I remember winning $2,500, but not what I spent it on. And the drinking. How did my liver survive? And Cher. We saw Cher, before her features became unrecognizable.

6

∞

Bride and groom flanked by my brothers and me. Fiftieth wedding anniversary. We got to give my mother the bride away. My younger brother handing her off to me, me handing her off to my older brother, my older brother likewise to my groom-again dad. She, happy as a lark, unaware we had slipped half a Valium into her orange juice that morning. He, nervous he'd flub his lines (my father hated orange juice; the other half of the Valium gone to waste). By the power vested in me, I pronounce you man and wife. My father could not have been happier, and it shows, the thing jumps out at you from the flat, two-dimensional surface of the photo, and he barely smiling. He died a month later. He'd been hiding the fact his insides had been bleeding themselves to death for nearly two years. Some sort of ulcerated tumor he'd tried to control by going vegetarian those same two years and trying to juice himself back to health. Some blamed it on his mulishness (he hated seeing doctors), some on old country ways (if you don't talk about the thing, the thing doesn't exist), some on that resigned response to providence, chance, what-have-you, he'd inherited from his Iberian ancestors by way of Puerto Rico. Not sure what to think. My father is dead six-years now and my mother's in a skilled-nursing facility, rehearsing familiar haunts ("*Me recuerdo la primera vez que tu papa me dirigió su palabra.*") on food the consistency of pap.

I opened the drawer for something, I was looking for something.

7

Patches

9C calls me Patches. "Hi, Patches, how you doing old boy?" I stretch and tilt my head up at him. I arch my back. I preen and I purr. I stretch my length against his leg. "Good old puss, knowing how to get what you want." He crouches and lets his hands play across the scruff of my back and across my belly as though I were a dog. People are such creatures of habit.

My previous owners named me Punch, but they moved away a few months before 9C moved in. He must have misheard one of the neighbors calling out to me, early morning, summer fog, like a voice in a tunnel. Or maybe it's the white patches at my neck and across my paws. It's better than Princess. What that idiot twenty-something neighbor of his in 5D calls me. If I knew he'd get it, I'd snarl something clever and cutting at him. He had a job once, several I think, but he always bounces back home and his mother always forgives him. I ignore him most days, as the rest of the neighbors do. "I'm not asking for a date, it's just a fucking movie for heaven's sake," he bellowed at 7E once. She smiled, said something about a boyfriend, and slammed the door in his face. I don't think he can help himself. I hear he takes anti-convulsive drugs to keep from falling down in the middle of a sentence, breaking things and flailing about like a dropped water hose. He takes another kind of pill to keep his mind from wandering like an abandoned dog, crossing the interstate to and from, trying to sniff his way home. He picks fights with the young woman with flame-colored hair and tank tops that barely cover her navel who rents the sofa bed in his mother's living room for so many pennies on the dollar and an egg sandwich for breakfast and lunch. She spends a lot of time talking to the device attached to her ear. She sighs and grimaces and exclaims dolefully to no one in particular, "I hate this place." He squanders his time fighting war games anonymously with people across the country. I don't think he quite recognizes who he is from day to day. His mother, a housewife all this life and possibly unto the next, rushes out of the house sometimes in curlers sometimes not and doesn't return for hours. His father, who doesn't live with them, dashes in, glares at everything within sight, and darts out again like a squirrel up a tree that's not his home.

9C may not know my real name but he knows better. He should, what with all those books on his shelf. He spends his days reading, occasionally looking up at the television he forgets to turn off. It's the hot season and he keeps the door open to let in stray breezes he hopes will cool his brow. He looks up after a few pages and smiles at me where I've stretched to catch the shade. He mouths the word Patches at me as though I can read lips. He won't let me into his place, believing no doubt that I'll shed on the furniture or piss on the carpet. I wouldn't, but he doesn't know that. He most certainly imagines I'm riddled with fleas, innocent of the fact I've charmed one of his other neighbors into changing my flea collar once a month. She'd let me in, sit awhile, but she has two cats of her own.

Sometimes I catch him napping, a book on his lap, a small pillow at his back. I wish I could teach him how to curl up on himself, nose to chest, so that he could smell his own comfort and drift off to the straightforward dreams of cats. "I bet you're dreaming of chasing mice, aren't you?" the woman with two cats told one of them once, stroking its nap as it dozed atop the windowsill. Why would it do that, I thought, when the real thing is in the bushes outside her window?

There are days when he keeps the blinds closed all day. I worry for him. I wonder what he's hiding from, keeping at bay, padding noiselessly in the near gloom. The world is just the world, and days are just days, I try to tell him, but he mistakes my sage counsel for a cry from an empty stomach, which he answers with a plate of snacks. Funny, I've never heard him stumble, cursing at a stubbed toe in the dark. Perhaps he's not as blind as I thought.

I brought him a field mouse once. He opened the door, jumped back and shouted, "Patches!"

I twitched my whiskers at him and pushed the treat toward him with my paw. "Take it," I meowed up at him. He made a face I've seen others make whenever I've done that. I nosed the mouse forward. "All right, all right, but don't make it a habit," he said. He went inside and came back with a stack of paper towels in his hand. The field mouse shuddered faintly as he grabbed it; he almost dropped it on top of my head. "Jesus, Patches, you could've at least taken him out of his misery." He looked at the bundle in his hand, which by then had stopped moving, and looked sad for a while. "I guess you think a thank you is in order." He nonetheless patted my head. He closed the door, and I could hear him walking off toward the kitchen. I hope he enjoyed the damned thing. It took me long enough; it kept

11

scurrying off into corners I could barely reach. I had to pretend I had forgotten it was there until it got up the nerve to scamper in the opposite direction; with one, two, three jumps and a few thumps against the floorboards I maneuvered it into my jaws. A spirited little thing, tried to nip at my whiskers until I snapped its back. I hope he liked it. They're much better when their blood is still warm.

I wrote him a poem.

Unclassified, an effective curse on one's behalf
Delivered to the heavens cold
Provides its undoing —
Better to
Be made
To
Last.
This
Proves
Patience
Ignorant
With promises kept
As poison to the heart is measured
In a luscious cup of mayhem made for one mad dunce.

"What's that you got stuck to your paw?" he said. "Let me see. The Maywood Classifieds. How'd you —?"

I suspect he never read it. Never once said whether it had the mark of genius or the makings of a hack. No appreciation these days I suppose for truly gifted art.

I brought him a pigeon. He made a face and let out a strange sound from the back of his throat. He slammed the door on

12

my face. Had he expected something bigger? In this neighborhood? (Granted, there are raccoons across the street in the alley behind the big empty warehouse, but they'll retreat only so far and leave big nasty gouges with their claws if you persevere, ragged grooves that tend to fester. I tried to warn Sesame the old tomcat down the block but he wouldn't listen. He hobbled for days, walked into a corner, closed his eyes and never came up from his nap. The old woman who normally fed him wailed when they came to take him away. She flailed and tore at her breast, as though she'd be allowed to keep him, as though Sesame had been such a prize. As though he'd committed to keeping her forever out of the old folk's home down the street, and now what? By then he was covered in ants, crawling things; not even the sewer rats would go near him.) A few minutes later, 9C came out with a broomstick and a large paper bag. He scooted the pigeon into the bag and for a moment there I thought, aha, he's come up with a new way of serving the thing. *Allez cuisinez.* Instead, he wrapped the top of the bag into a tight knot, walked to the dumpster around back and threw the thing in. I was most terribly offended, but then I thought, maybe he hasn't developed a taste for urban fowl. Yet, here was the perfect opportunity to educate his palate. Terribly offended.

"You naughty cat," stamping his foot. I hissed back. No point in insulting the guest because you didn't like what he brought as an appetizer. "Nasty, nasty, nasty," he said. I arched my back, tossed up my tail. He's lucky I wasn't a skunk.

"Where have you been, you old puss," he said. He had snuck up on me when I was drowsing. "Did you go on vacation or something? I thought I'd lost you." He nuzzled me against his cheek. I couldn't help myself and purred back.

I had kept my distance for weeks. You'd have thought with

13

all the books he read, with all the big thoughts he thought, he would have gotten the point of a good object lesson. But you never know sometimes with some people. I'm going to have to sneak into his place and take a good look at what he's been reading. Cats never go on vacation; our whole lives are a kind of vacation. He'd have known that had he read the right books.

My previous owners moved to Chicago. "Wish we could take you with us Punch," the female told me, "but you're an outside cat, an L.A. cat, we don't think you'll get used to the snow." "We'll figure something out," the male this time, "we'll find someone special for you." No thank you, I thought, I'm too old to be palmed off to the first bidder. And how did they know I wouldn't have gotten used to snow? I could get used to anything; I got used to living with their piebald dog and idiot children. I hid behind the dumpster for a week prior to their move, caught mice for dinner, drank run-off from the sprinklers, and wouldn't answer their calls. "What are we going to do?" the female cried. "Leave him, what else can we do." "But what's he going to do without us?" As though they weren't going to leave me anyway, as though I wasn't going to have to fend for myself. I don't think they ever got used to my independence, wanting me to curl up next to them all the time, follow them around the house, if only with my eyes, beg them for dinner, a little coochy coo coochy coo isn't he preciouswecious night and day until on midnight ramble I missed the litter box, what a ruckus, and by not even an inch or two. Now, more than half of the building feeds me, morning, noon and night, anytime I so much as yawn. How's that for an L.A. cat!

In any case, I've decided to adopt 9C; he spends too much time with himself. We all need someone special to worry about, and to worry about us. He stays up reading until past

14

my late-night stroll, and sleeps in. Someone is always trying to sell him something. He hangs up using language that sears even my street-smart ears as I try to snooze outside his door. He's been looking for a job for a while, but no one's biting. He wears hats indoors, sometimes backwards; he has a collection of them; I'm not sure who he's trying to impress. He whistles, dances with his shadow, dawdles. He complains to a friend that calls every other day that the more time he spends alone the more he keeps losing a connection to something vital. "I hate how everything feels inauthentic," he tells his friend. "You have to be blind, even to your own duplicity, to qualify as a human being these days," he adds. Do you see why I worry about him? All that time alone has affected him, generating queer echoes in his head. I think what's missing is a type of indifference, a quality of being necessary to get along in the world, to adapt, adjust, absolve, carry on. Few friends come to visit.

He likes to talk to the guy across the way, sports, local politics, tequila stories, ruined honeymoons, magazine articles on obscure subjects. 2B is from another country, so 9C attributes what he misunderstands or easily misconstrues to a loss in translation, a failure of the tongue to land on the right word or the ear on the right level of understanding. They smile a lot, somewhat formal, somewhat shy, and shrug their shoulders across a gulf 9C would call cultural but that I consider human.

For a while, a handsome chocolate-colored girl with tight curls in her hair would come by once a week. For a while, he would open the door, they would smile at each other and hug and he'd invite her in. For a while, he would cook for her or they would order in. For a while, their conversation would ring off the walls like a smattering of rain. Laughter would follow. I liked her. "This is Patches," he said the first time, introducing us. "I'm allergic to cats," she said, although she didn't scurry away. She had the same color eyes as mine, and stood there, onyx-eyed, and let him groom me for a while. She must have moved to Chicago, too; for the snow, I suppose. I wonder if I could talk him into taking a trip with me.

Sometimes I let him chase me around the small paved-over courtyard as if I'm afraid of him. I hide behind one of the steps of the apartment unit. He pretends he's lost track of me. I feign a snarl, appropriate to my size, and pounce from behind. He chases me some more. I wonder if he thinks I'm a strange-looking dog. If one day he tosses a Frisbee at me, I swear I'll scratch him.

"Let me in, let me lounge on that cushy chair, sit a spell, stretch awhile."

He lets me in.

"There that's better," I said, getting settled. "I think you're as compulsive about your doubts as I am about mice."

"What do you mean?"

"You've been dining out on your fears and suspicions for so long you've started to believe they're a crucial part of your diet."

"I don't think you understand. I don't think I understand."

It wasn't how I had planned the conversation in my head, I'd gone in too fast, too deep, had left no room to maneuver, a transcendent path forward, tit for tat, ambiguity and paradox, unguided tours in time and space, salience and its polar opposite.

I started over. "How about them Dodgers?"

"First MLB team to open an office in Asia, but other than that."

"It's the pitching staff. It's always the pitching staff."

"Would you like some milk?" He pointed toward the kitchen,

16

as though he expected me to go fetch it. He does think I'm a dog.

"Let's hold off. I'm beginning to think I'm lactose intolerant."

"We were talking existential junctures, signature events, ordeals in Texas light."

"We were? I thought we were past that. I thought we were onto the higher mathematics of the curveball?"

"Levels of the game, levels of the game."

"Now we're talking."

"People take on the color of their surroundings and when you're no longer in them you feel drained out."

"You lost your job, yes. Sesame said something about that. But that was months ago? What with him being gone and all. Months ago."

"That's just it, I never liked my job. Jobs. Any of them. Joked about it all the time."

"And now the joke's on you."

"That wasn't very polite. You're a guest in my house."

"You like reading books, don't you? You do it all the time. Turning pages, highlighting phrases, paragraphs, picking one off the shelf, putting it back, picking another, turning more pages. Sometimes you have two or three on your lap. Sometimes you talk back to them. Do something related to books."

"I like daydreaming. And pasta. Doesn't pay the rent."

"Forget about the rent. Be like me — enjoy the weather, the sun on your back, people feeding you all the time."

"I'm not as cute as you are; people will forget to feed me on schedule. Plus I don't think I could ever get used to the feel of asphalt on my paws."

"There's a lot of grass out there, yours for the asking."

"What would I do about my books?"

17

"Wouldn't need them, trust me. You'd be surprised what you learn when you're out in the world, what people tell you for a couple of meows and a rub against their ankles."

"How would I remember anything? My memory's like a sieve."

"Training, like spitting out hairballs. I remember the first limerick I was ever told.

> 'There once was a wolf high up in China,
> Striped, short-tailed, intermittent angina.
> In deep sleep he thought he smelled sheep
> So he spent all his dreamtime trying to find them.'"

"That's pretty bad."

"She meant well. Never stifle the creativity of a sixty-five year old, the potential for growth."

"I'm trying to be serious here."

"Bet Kafka had fun now and then. Bet Camus was a hoot in his off hours."

"Now you're being jejune."

"Quick get the dictionary!"

"I could get angry you know, not feed you for a while."

"Now *that* would be serious."

"We seem to have come to a crossroads."

"My point exactly."

Loud, uneven hammering sounded through one of the walls off the dining room, what passed for a dining room in such cramped quarters. Someone was trying to nail something together.

"He does that all the time, sometimes late into the night. I complain but he starts up again a couple of days later. He's

18

a little driven. Keeps talking about rain, forty days and forty nights. It's a bachelor apartment. Whatever it is I don't think he'll ever get it out the door." The hammering started again, stopped and started, out of plan. The man didn't know what he was doing.

"If I behave myself can we start over?"

He sounded earnest, self-consciously tucking his feet beneath the reclining chair, aware of a sudden that he was the only man in the room barefoot.

"Some people die of insomnia," I confessed. "I'll do anything to get some sleep. Go ahead. "

"I believe in mom, apple pie and the American way. I believe in mankind's beleaguered steps toward his, okay, her own humanity. I believe that God is more than a concept and less than a white-bearded old man on a fiery throne waiting to answer our prayers. I believe that history turns in directions that don't always point forward. I believe that evolution, the universe, someone, invented human emotions to keep us humble. I believe in peace in our lifetime, any time. I believe that twenty-twenty hindsight is designed to allow us to eavesdrop on ourselves. I believe some major event in the history of the Jehovah's Witness is about to come true. I believe that people who blame everyone but themselves exhibit a signal instance of a lack of imagination. I believe Shakespeare has been over interpreted and that Nietzsche is a bore. I believe that beauty is in the eye of the beholder except when it isn't. I believe the family and not the individual is the basic unit of civilization. I believe the children are our future, teach them well and they will light the way, except of course that they won't."

"I had eight more lives before I walked into this."

"You said surprise me. I was being polite."

"No, no, I think I'm the one being polite. But go on."

"Let's see, I've told you about my mother and father and my brother, who have I left out? Ah, yes, my sister. My sister used to tell her dolls stories aloud when she thought no one was listening. On the seventh day of the seventh week of the seventh month, a young man entered Heaven's Gate without his sunglasses. Someone had convinced him he wouldn't need them. ... She was known as Mademoiselle Coquette because her eyes always seemed to beckon. No one suspected it was a nervous tic. ... We are talking Mitteleuropa here, Slavs, Slovenes, Poles, Czechs, where husbands sleep with their goats instead of their wives, to get in a good morning's milking. ... The Cardinal, because of his unusually small feet, especially for someone of his rank and demeanor, had to buy his leather-shod sandals at a specialty shop off one of the major arteries in the Township of S., population thirteen hundred. His handsome, piano-prone hands were a different story. ... And then there was the one about a sea-serpent and a browbeaten prince and a misguided sorcerer's apprentice and a misnamed princess, but that was darker, less forgiving of anyone who played a major role in the narrative, not a good week for her I suppose. Oh how those dolls listened to everything she said; you would have thought they were her real family. My sister and I are very much alike, Patches, except I'm taller. She eloped at the age of sixteen. It wasn't until after the death of her umpteenth marriage that she came back to us. But she came back different. When I asked her once for old times' sake if she'd tell me one of the stories she used to tell her dolls, she looked at me as if she couldn't remember who I was, as if I had the wrong sister in mind, as though the possibility that we were related was a monumental blunder. Then she started to talk about her 401k plan, pension

20

rules, lower earnings estimates, fees and exemptions, the need to stay diversified, to plan ahead. I realized she thought I was one of her dolls and that she was trying to get me to fall asleep by telling me one of her stories, a more up-to-date one. I liked the childhood ones better. I told her so. 'Shush already,' she said. 'Let me think. I'm trying not to repeat myself.'"

… dreaming of Chicago, where we all live, the wind off the lake, the large pizza-eating mice and the cats who chased after them, Sailor Roo, the chocolate-brown girl from Compton. I'm asleep already, why is my sister still talking?

"I once had a cat named Patches."

Lorca at Five O'Clock in the Afternoon

You live and you die.

All right, all right, there's a lot of living to be done in between, choices to be made, dreams to be fulfilled, and much else, but there's no use denying those bookends.

Sorry, it's that kind of day and I'm in that kind of mood. I'm trying my best, but everywhere I look memories threaten.

The front wall of my bedroom is floor-to-ceiling glass. From it you'd see the city but for that damned tree, its massive back toward me, weeping endless leaves onto the ceiling of the first level. What's left is a pinch of sky, and turning sideways, over the shoulder of the building, a glimpse of my neighbor's front yard. A closed system, a window without space to see, a good eye with a patch over it.

I often wonder why I bother to open the curtains; but I keep the windows always so clean, hoping someday for the sound of chainsaws.

I should get up, do the dishes, mop the kitchen floor or dust the already sparkling furniture. Few ghosts linger in the ordinary. Although not here. Not here.

"Only mystery enables us to live." From a diary entry, I believe, I don't know enough about the man. "Only mystery."

Which was fitting, Lorca to my father, one longtime dead, another about to be buried, one mystery compounded by another. But he had been my father's favorite poet, and I am supposed to find something suitable to read at his funeral, one last wish, bequeathed to yours truly, because my father knew I would not say no to a last wish, to any of his wishes, there had been so few between us.

Mystery and death, death and mystery.

La muerte
entra y sale
y sale y entra
la muerte
de la taberna

— when all I want is to celebrate a life. Isn't that what quiet words at a graveside are supposed to be about? The lingering portrait, the gesture or smile that will never be forgotten, the sound of laughter in a room, the quickness of a stride, the smell of the familiar on all the shirts left behind — my father's laughter, his stride, his smell.

Get up, get up, get up. The funeral is in a couple of hours — at five in the afternoon; Lorca triumphs again! — and here I am unable to move a muscle to hurry it along.

In the bathroom, turning on lights, I remember my father's first reaction to the room. "That's an awfully big mirror for just one person — my God, it's obscene. How can you stand seeing yourself naked in that thing? How do you hide anything from it?"

"Dad, it came with the place."

"Jesus, I'd have to learn to shave in the dark!"

Downstairs, he'd peered into the sundeck, squinting at what little light bled through the screen of leaves.

"When do you think the car will be ready?"

"You don't have to do this, you know," my father said. "I can borrow a car from someone else."

"No, no, I was just wondering. Don't worry about me, I'll manage."

"It shouldn't take long," from Tito my cousin, who along with my other cousin had driven my father over.

"We're waiting for a part." Gelo, this time, dressed in overalls and greased to the elbows from working on cars all day long. "Place is nice — you live here by yourself?" Walking around the living room, hands nervously working behind him, afraid to touch anything.

Tito nodded. "Nice, nice."

"Had a roommate, but he moved to Houston about three weeks ago," I said. "Anybody for some coffee, I was just about to make some?"

"No time — we gotta go." My father, insistent as always.

"The hell with that, I'm tired. And that was a lot of stairs. I'll take some."

"Me too. Make it strong."

"Ah, hell," my father said, slumping onto the cane rocker. The same cane rocker he would always fall into whenever he came over, which was rare enough and mostly my mother's doing. Their visits would be short, the hour a minor ordeal. She would do most of the talking. Sitting on the rocker, legs crossed, hand

25

to chin, my father would nod now and then as though on a lesson well learned. Across from him, I'd surprise myself hand to chin, legs crossed, nodding at nothing, and ever so slightly, so as not to be caught, would shift to another position. That was one mirror I did not want to look into.

Maybe I'll sneak in Neruda or Vallejo or Juan Ramón Jiménez or some other Hispanic, all of them with death seemingly on their lips all the time, who'd know the difference.

Sólo el muerto. Sólo el muerto.

My father, of course, would know the difference.

Death will come and will have your eyes —
this death which attends us
from morning to night, sleepless,
deaf, like an old remorse
or absurd vice.

Surely, he'd like the mordant pleasantries of that one, even if from an old reprobate like Pavese.

No, I suppose I shouldn't chance it, there were too many misgivings between the two of us already. I'd never hear the end of it.

∞

When my father spoke Spanish to my mother, especially when he thought we weren't listening and he would tire of his usual perorations, he would all of a sudden acquire a lisp, como un Castellano. The nuns at his school, to which he went until he was twelve, the year his parents died six months apart and he had to start fending for himself, would have it no other way. La lengua Borinqueña, the one with which the children

26

entered their classrooms, was an affront to the delicate hearing of women who, outside of the grinding duty of caring for unruly children six hours a day, seven days a week, endlessly putting up with their vulgar cries and crude exclamations, were only used to listening to themselves talk to God in nightly prayer. In speaking to the Almighty, one not only had to have the right words to say, but also learn to pronounce them properly. I wonder if in the silence of compliant prayer, upon knees raw from protracted kneeling, when the lack of sleep and constant fasting would start to take their toll, from time to time atop the susurration of island winds and the whisper of tropical mosquitoes these women imagined the voice of God answering their entreaties gently but insistently with "*Has esto Sor Rosa y tu aquello Sor Betilde*," como un Castellano. And if their Heavenly Father spoke to them like a Castilian, who were they not to return the favor by speaking back to him in His own tongue?

When the sisters asked one of their charges to recite from memory one of the poems they would struggle to drum into their heads, and the reluctant child would forget himself and a recalcitrant tongue would do its bidding, they would fish a shimmering penny from some hidden pocket in their habits and send the kid off to the chapel to deposit the precious coin into the hands of Nuestro Padre Jesucristo o su Madre la Santa María or if they were intrepid to the greater Christ-on-the-Cross.

Late at night, when everyone else was asleep, my father would get up, sneak to the mirror in the hallway and school his diction, ready and ramrod, as if to a roomful of expectant children. Proper diction, he would tell himself, proper diction. For that, he would get an extra penny, his to keep, his to spend on whatever antojito would suit him.

27

When I'm by myself
your ten years remain with me,
the three blind horses,
your fifteen faces with the face of the stoning
and the tiny frozen fevers on the leaves of corn.
Stanton, my son, Stanton.
At twelve midnight the cancer left the corridors
speaking with the empty snails of the documents,
the cancer springing to life,
full of clouds and thermometers
with the chaste longing of the apple to be pecked by
nightingales.

That's what they had taught him. That's what he had learned.

∞

I just want to say a few words about my father. I'm not going to take long, just the words of a son too numb to say much but too angry not to attempt to say something. I'm not angry at my father; mostly at myself. But I'll get to that in a moment.

My father was a man of few words, terse, economical, to the point. Not that he couldn't talk when he wanted to, for as long as he wanted to, on any subject that exercised him — say, baseball or the current president — but he was a man who knew himself too well ever want to hear the sound of his own voice just because he could.

What I'm going to talk about is why I'm angry — and again, mostly at myself. When I would call the house and he would answer the phone — which was rare, since he let my mother answer the phone — we would always, and I mean always, talk about four things: how was I doing, how was my job, how was my car, and was I paying my bills on time? Over and again, for

28

the last thirty or so many years since I moved out of the house: how was I doing, how was my job, how was my car, and was I paying my bills on time? Okay, recently he threw in a fifth subject: he wanted to make sure, he insisted, he was adamant, that I shouldn't vote for the current president in the coming election!

In any case, what I'm angry about — the great, dumb, mean tragedy in my relationship with my father — was that because he was a man of such few words, at least with me, I never sat him down and talked to him about his life. I never got to ask him why he thought he had become the man he was, why he had made the choices he had made, why he decided to marry my mother, why he kept loving her more and more each day of the fifty-five years they lived together, why he had decided to come to America, what he thought of the life he had built for his family here, why he had worked one job for most of his life, why he had had three sons, what he thought of our lives, had they turned out the way he had wanted them to turn out, had the choices he made — for he came to America to make a better life for us all — panned out in the lives he thought we were living, was he proud of the fact that I have done fairly well in my life, that I've always had jobs that (for the most part) I've enjoyed, that my cars have always run well, and that, yes, I've always (again for the most part) paid my bills on time, and that, no, I was not going to vote for the current president in the coming election.

What I'm upset about, what truly saddens me is that because I didn't sit him down and force him to talk to me, really talk to me about his life, I'll never have a handle on him.

What I realize now is that what made him distinctive, what made him remarkable as a man, as a father and a husband, was the way he talked. Not just the sound of his voice, which was remarkable enough, but the words he used and the expressions he employed — laconic, measured, droll. My father, as most of you can attest to, had a great sense of humor, brash, sometimes downright foulmouthed. And because when occasionally — and it was mostly, unfortunately, only occasionally — when we did sit down to talk, he had a lot of good stories to tell of growing up poor and an orphan in Puerto Rico, of how he and my Tío Pancho took care of each other after their parents died much too early and much too young, what they learned and taught each other about growing up, getting along in the world, becoming men, being husbands and fathers, of joining the Army when he did, of his experiences in boot camp in Texas, of falling in love with my mother and wooing her until he convinced her to marry him, of being proud to be Borinqueño, proud to be an American, so many other things.

What I'm going to miss most about my father is that I don't have enough of him in my ear, the sound and swing of him, to remember in the coming years. I should have made him talk to me more, I should have forced him to tell me more stories, I should have made him fill my ears with the memory of him, with enough words to fill my brain with his voice for the rest of the time I have here on earth. So, Papi, please forgive me. Next time — and there will be a next time, because we're going to meet again — I'm going to make you talk, and talk, and talk, until you run out of words. Until then, hasta luego, Papi.

∞

One last betrayal.

I couldn't do it. I couldn't bring myself to read from Lorca, not at the church service at least. All those dour sepulchral images under lowering arches and the omnipresent stained glass — it would have been too much. Maybe later on, at the graveside, the sky would swallow up the words, and I could pretend I hadn't said them.

To William Carlos Williams a poem is a capsule within which we wrap our punishable secrets. I keep re-reading Lorca, trying desperately to uncover his secrets, punishable or not, and therefore my father's. And if speech is the soul in action, then I rarely got to glimpse my father's, or he mine, for we seldom talked.

"Is there anyone else that would like to say a few, parting words?"

I can't. The mind balks and stutters, the tongue frozen in place. Lorca was your constant companion, not mine.

"All right then." The man in the dark gray suit, whom the funeral home retained for such services, takes something from his breast pocket and comes toward my mother.

"On behalf of the President of the United States," he intones, "I would like to present you with this token of his appreciation for the services your husband provided his nation in a time of need."

It's some kind of medal, which my mother hesitates to take. It is too much a closing gesture; she would actually have to let go.

He turns to me, and I take it from his hand. What choice do I have? I begin to weep at last, even after I had promised myself I wouldn't.

∞

"We have to talk." Jaime, my older brother.

I'd seen him approach Tomas earlier. Tomas had dismissed him with a wave of a hand and a snort of displeasure. And now he is after me.

"Can't this wait?" We were at my parents' house, where I

was trying to nurse my sense of failure.

"I'm sorry, we can't. We have to square accounts."

"What accounts?"

"You don't think all of this came free?" He's cornered me in father's bedroom, where he'd spent the last years of his life, after my parents had stopped sleeping together, his restlessness and her snoring, after fifty-five years, having worn out their welcome. "The church service, the floral arrangements, the body back and forth from the funeral home to the church, all of it, even the pastor. And we had to upgrade the casket; it was nothing but a wooden box when the whole thing started."

"I thought mom and dad had made those arrangements a long time ago — what happened?"

I pace in a space with little room to maneuver. I keep bumping into what remains of my father's last years, and I'm overcome by a sense of intrusion. Jaime's by the door, blocking my way of escape.

"That's what I thought, too. But they were sold the bare minimum. We couldn't very well leave it like that."

"That's hard to believe." My parents were nobody's fool. "They must have wanted things a certain way — why couldn't you leave well enough alone?"

"That's not the point anymore." The recognizable tick above his left brow, with which we are both familiar, is throbbing like a small wound or false pride. "Sara and I have spent a lot of money making sure everything would run smoothly the last two days, and we still have repairs to the house we haven't gotten to, and it's all well and good 'Leave well enough alone' but who was going to make sure the body got picked up, that the services came off on time, you know how Dad was about these things, the floral arrangements, the pictures we collected

32

and mounted at the church and the funeral home, the music and hymns, who the pallbearers were going to be, Mom and Dad hadn't thought about that, and Tomas was flying in from Florida and you were busy consoling Mom, do you think these things arranged themselves, or that they were given to us for free? We just got the house, and even though —"

"Stop, just stop. I can't think about these things right now."

"You just don't want to. And neither does Tomas. Both of you, tears and sorrow, tears and sorrow. How very Hispanic of you."

"Will you please just stop."

"The difference is $8,000. Sara and I are willing to put up most of it, since I'm the oldest. I figure you and Tomas should come up with —."

"No."

"What?"

"You heard me."

"What does that mean?"

"I'm not sure. What I do know is that I'm not going to talk about this any longer — not with you or anyone else. Get out of my way."

"You can't do this, Paulito."

"Just watch."

"Paul, this is our father we're talking about."

"I know who the fuck we're talking about — where do you think I've been for the last few days? I'll pay my respects to him in my own way and in my own time. Now, get the hell out of my way!"

I rush out of the room. To the welcoming arms of my mother, brows deeply furrowed. Normally her features are quiet and serene, the bangs on her brow soothing like a balm.

"He means well, you know?" Patting my arm as she would my father's whenever he was angry.

"Not well enough," wincing at her touch. "I need some air."

Tomas rushes after me. Tomas the half-changeling, with a fullback's great broad shoulders and developing girth, and Nordic complexion, unlike the rest of us, but with enough of our quirks and idiosyncrasies for people to hazard que si, que era de la familia, what else could he be?

"What did he say? He kept trying to talk to me but I wouldn't let him. What's he up to?"

"You'll know soon enough; it'll be your turn next."

"I'll kick his ass if he fucks with me today."

"Oh, great, just what we need to complete the day — a scene."

"It's what we Hispanics do best."

"Not this Hispanic. And we're called Latinos nowadays, remember?"

"Yeah, well fuck that, too. Dad hated that term."

"He was from a different generation. And it's not as if he's around to lecture us on the fine points of cultural nomenclature."

"You never know. He could be listening to us right now. And don't go using fancy words on me to try and change the subject — you sound just like him when you do that."

"Do not."

"Do too."

"Fuck you."

"Fuck you back with a baseball bat."

Our laughter echoes and booms on the busy street. I should have never taught him that when he was five years old and me six years his senior. I should have known better.

I love my taller younger brother with an intensity bordering

34

on the miraculous. With Jaime, things were more complicated. We were born twelve months apart, too close for comfort, living almost parallel lives, mostly a sense of claustrophobia in each other's company.

"Come on," he says, "let's go for a walk."

"We're supposed to be entertaining guests."

"And putting up with their condolences. Jaime's taken care of everything else; let him take care of that, too."

We set off, trading stories of our father's legendary hearing — at least where we were concerned. He was renowned for playing sordo y mudo when my mother would want him to do something he didn't agree with. "¿Que? ¿Qué quieres que haga ahora?" But when it came to his children, we could be in another state or sending messages to each other underground and he'd figure out what we were up to. "I heard that." "No, you can't, so forget about it." And if he was truly pissed that we were trying to get anything past him: "No me hagan pasar por pendejo." We kept few secrets when my father was around, and even when he wasn't.

"We should be getting back," Tomas says after a while.

"Let me ask you something."

"Sure," turning toward me.

"What happened to him? What do you think made him that way?"

"You mean Dad, don't you?" He puts a hand on the nape of my neck. "Paulito, Dad was just Dad. He was never anyone else but."

"Yes, but —"

"Stop it. You keep turning things over all the time. One of these days you're not going to like what you find. Let it go."

We walk back to the house in silence. What could he mean?

35

What was the point of life if you couldn't look at it from as many angles as you could afford?

My mother comes out to greet us. Most of the guests are gone, and I'm glad I don't have to pretend I'm the strong one, for anyone's sake.

"We went for a walk," I declare guiltily before she can say anything.

"You said that earlier."

"Where's Jaime?" Tomas asks.

"He left a while ago, after he stopped waiting for the two of you to come back." She squeezes herself between the two of us, trying to put her arms around us as best she can. "He was pretty angry — whether at the two of you or at himself, I can't be sure."

"I'll go call him and apologize." Tomas heads inside the house.

"Come on, I'll make you a little *chocolatito*, the way you always like it."

In the kitchen, she reaches into a drawer below the counter.

"Here, I'm sure he would have wanted you to have this."

A sepia-colored photograph of him in uniform, taken in Texas at the beginning of the Korean War, a graceful mustache magically suspended between the bottom curve of the nose and the upper lip. It must have taken him hours of disciplined care to situate it just so, a streak of splendor over such stern lips, with the kind of straight razors they issued army boys those days. The military dress cap sits at a rakish angle, as if winking at the camera. What could he have found so terribly amusing, going off to war? "*Travieso, tu papa era muy travieso*," my mother once said.

That mustache and those eyes, it was easy to see why she fell in love with him.

36

∞

Five o'clock, Lorca's least favorite time of day, a time of indolence and indiscretion, the Spanish sun languid against the sky.

At five in the afternoon,
It was exactly five in the afternoon.
A boy brought the white sheet
at five in the afternoon.
A basketful of lime in readiness
at five in the afternoon
Beyond that, death and death alone
at five in the afternoon. ...
Horrifying five in the afternoon!
The stroke of five on every clock.
The dark of five in the afternoon.

More than once my father made it quite clear that when he died he wanted to be buried at five in the afternoon. He found the hour, as he found Lorca's rhymes and meters, formative and emblematic. Every day after he'd retired, until his legs could no longer sustain him, he would go out for an afternoon walk at precisely 4:30 p.m. A half hour's walk that would have him arriving back home at exactly five o'clock in the afternoon. He would stop for a moment, turn toward the remaining light of day and bow as if in assent. To what or to whom, he would never say. He would knock on the door three times like some old fashioned gentlemen-caller come a'courting, until my mother would let him in, coffee cup in hand. He would retire to one corner of the room, where he would finish the day's paper, front to back, before asking for his dinner. One day, one more day, he must have thought, without someone at the door, rushing to bring white sheets, baskets full of limes at the ready.

So here it is five o'clock, and here am I at this strange hour and at this strange place, bounded by willows and poplars indifferent in their winter sleep, buckeye, deer weed, and foothill ash struggling against steep inclines. A chill is seeping up through my shoes from months of arctic weather, and everywhere I turn, I'm surrounded by stiff flat inarticulate islands of regimented tombstones. I hardly dare move. So much serenity and stillness must be jarring even to the dead.

If my father wanted us, his auditors at graveside, to locate him in Lorca's slender hesitancies or wider certainties, why didn't he leave a better roadmap: read this poem first, and then this other one, read this line and then the following one? It's like standing before the world's largest floor plan with the "You are here" forever shifting place every time you spot it.

> Listen, my son: the silence.
> It's a rolling silence,
> a silence,
> where slip valleys and echoes,
> bending foreheads
> down toward the ground.

Okay, old man, I'm listening. Crouched on both knees, ear to gravestone, I'm listening. And so will you. Even if through the words of a long dead poet, one with whom I have little in common, but the same can be said of you, the same can be said of you.

That's not true. They say I have your sense of humor, wintry, triggering, your unerring sense of justice, and your unlimited love of books, their song and their savor, their buzz and their thrills, their booming secrets and hushed blatancies.

My father's life, is a presence forever present, forbidding and elusive but always stubbornly *there*, the long Iberian forehead and sharp nose lovely in profile. Lovely and terrifying and heartbreaking in ways I'm still trying to come to terms with. His is a life in parenthesis, and how am I supposed to go on when I don't know what happened before or after? How am I supposed to know what I've lost?

"We Latins want sharp profiles and visible mystery. Form and sensuality," wrote Lorca in 1928. All I have of my father is the visible mystery. Form and sensuality he kept for himself and my mother.

My father had once been a wandering minstrel. Up and down the coastline of the island, from busy squalid sidewalks to sparse and shapeless townhall squares. One of the many jobs he'd had before he settled down and became an honest man. "*Un jíbaro con guitarra, un pela'o sin fortuna, pero comí y sobreviví,*" he'd told my mother. Even as two more of his siblings died of malnutrition and ill care. I can't imagine this entirely too-somber man entertaining anyone for his supper, delighted people would pay him to be amused for an hour or so. He never sang for us. He had survived, and that had been enough.

Mystery and death, death and mystery. Even from the grave, he sends me back to Lorca. So be it.

> *Once I had a son name John.*
> *Once I had a son. ...*
> *I saw him playing on the last raised step of*
> *the Mass and he lowered a tin bucket*

39

into the priest's deep heart.
I pounded on the coffin.
My son! My son! My Son! ...
If my boy had been a bear,
I wouldn't fear the crocodiles lying in ambush
or have seen the sea lashed to the trees
for the brutal pleasure of the regiments.
If only my son had been a bear! ...
Once he had a son.
A son! A son! A son
who was his alone, because he was his son!
His son! His son! His son!

I cried for my father, would he have cried for me? His son, his son, his son. I wish I had been born a bear.

Middlemarch

Time, time, time, is on my side, yes it is. What's your name? (what's your name?). Who's your daddy? (who's your daddy?). (He rich) Is he rich like me? Has he taken (has he taken) any time (any time) (to show) to show you what you need to live? If I could save time in a bottle, the first thing that I'd like to do. Lying in my bed I hear the clock tick and think of you. Caught up in circles confusion is nothing new. But I'm talking to myself again, stalling for ... ha, ha ... Wonder if I keep this up, I'll eventually start to make sense?

∞

Why won't you let me in? Why won't you play the game?

Why should I? Play the game? Let you in?

Because it's all a game, always has been, always will be. And because if I'm not in I'm out.

So this is about you?

Doesn't have to be. It can be about us.

You believe that, don't you?

Always has been, always will be.

I was lying, of course — but only about the last part.

Or was I lying to myself?

∞

I'm forgetting a million things I'm supposed to do today. One: Call the manager and tell her the waste disposal isn't working — again. Two: Call the dentist's office and change my appointment for tomorrow. Three: Call the unemployment office and update my status. Four: Call the bank's automated call center to make sure my last few checks have gone through and confirm the balance on my account. Five: Call the car dealer and make an appointment for tomorrow to get my breaks checked, now I've cancelled my dental appointment. Six: Call his mother, call his sister, call his brother, call his other brother, call the fire department, call the police, call the heavens for help because he's got too many calls to make in one day and he's sure to forget the order of magnitude, precedence, what-have-you. He begins to panic. He's beginning to refer to himself in the third person, more often than not, and that can't be good. Seven: Turn off the laptop, the iPod, the mp3 player, the Xbox, pick up the phone, damn you, pick up the phone.

∞

The world is meaningfully structured. I read something about that the other day and started to believe it. Something's wrong here. Can't be me, must be you. Areas of effect, areas of influence, shared and unshared inferences, explanation as argument, argument as explanation. The world is meaningfully structured. Something's wrong here. Can't be me, must be you.

∞

Since I can do no good because a woman / Reach constantly at something that is near it, he said, absently hugging himself, as if cold.

Meaning he's starting to re-read *Middlemarch* again, which I know makes him despondent. The unexpected shiver... — well I'm not sure what that means, except that we were in for a long night.

42

But that's a reverse image; I've reversed the image. It was me who'd begun to re-read *Middlemarch*, and it was he who was in for a long night.

I always did know how to lie to mirrors.

∞

I shall never love again.

I shall never lie again.

I shall never let someone make love or lie to me again.

I shall never pretend I know whereof I speak. Again.

∞

It goes without saying, you said.

Look, you said.

You're doing this on purpose, you said.

I have no idea, you said.

Humor me, you said.

I can't very well put that into a wheelbarrow, you said.

Don't you see, you said.

Sure it does, you said.

Ah, come on, you said.

Time will tell, you said.

How's that possible? you said.

A deal breaker, you said.

Unforeseen consequences, you said.

I couldn't care less, you said.

How would you know? you said.

A private truth and a public lie, you said.

Talk to me, I said. Just talk to me.

∞

I ask you, was it worth it?

You don't answer. You lie there, back to me, naked, refusing a blanket, your gym-built ass like the last best bite of a scoop of ice cream, the turn of your spine treasuring the slightest of shivers. Hands on your lap, palms up, you seem intent on measuring out your lifeline, top to bottom, beginning to end. We hadn't been together that long before I learned that pose, hands on your lap, palms up, gauging the future. That small tremor meant that what you saw was more of the same.

We're in this for all the wrong reasons.

So you keep telling me, and yet here we are.

Why do you stay?

Because it explains something.

What's that?

That the universe's not as fucked up as we think it is.

Want to know why I stay?

You shift your shoulders this way and shift them back. How I wish I could forget how much I knew you.

The day you were born is, was, my lucky number — how fucked up is that?

People marry for less, I say.

And go mad and bury their wives in the back yard for the dogs to dig up.

You get up and head to the bathroom. As usual, you couldn't hold your water.

Or so I thought. I fell asleep. Past midnight, another dawn, another beginning, hours away. That was the last time I saw you, except perhaps for that one time at 3rd Street Promenade, when all I could do was nod. What was the point of pretending that somewhere on that lifeline, had you clasped it to mine, there had been room for a happy ending?

Lou

Lord, he's got that sweet something, and I told my gal friend

Lou.

He got that sweet something, and I told my gal friend

Lou.

From the way she's been a'ravin', she must have gone and tried it

too.

I am embarrassed to say that once or twice, when I was younger and didn't know any better, and once when I was older and should have, I was someone's guy friend Lou.

Souvenir

My mother groaned, my father wept,
Into the dangerous world I leapt;
Helpless, naked, piping loud,
Like a fiend hid in a cloud.

Struggling in my father's hands,
Striving against my swaddling bands;
Bound and weary I thought best
To sulk upon my mother's breast.

Who writes these things? A book's worth.

I thought about you when I bought it, I said. That's okay, no need to thank me. Just thought it would be better than a beer mug with the state's name written across it.

Crocodile Tears

The heart is a lonely hunter.
The hunter is a lonely heart.
The heart is.
The hunter is.
Lonely is.
The is.
Is is.

$$\infty$$

Are you lonesome tonight?
Do you miss me tonight?
Are you sorry we drifted apart?
Is your heart filled with pain, shall I come back again?
Tell me dear, are you lonesome tonight?

By the Sea, By the Sea, By the ...

"It couldn't have been that bad," the sea-dragon said, rearing its silver-backed neck, as though to let out a crick. Satisfied, it let its massive head rest on its large fin-like paws. It was, for the moment, a most civilized creature.

"Well ..." said the young mage, "Now that you mention it."

"Which I did."

The young mage scowled down at the sea-dragon from his perch on the bluff and stared out into the sky. Whatever was there refused to take the bait. "I thought this was going to be a friendly conversation."

"What do you mean?" the sea-dragon protested, training its spellbinding bottle-green eyes on the mage. "I agreed with you."

"Tone is as telling as words."

"My apologies, I'm used to eating wizards not having heartfelt conversations with them. I must be out of practice."

"I'm the one who should apologize. It's just that ... I'm not used to failing, not used to swallowing my pride."

"Swallowing — I'm absolutely all for it. One must chew one's food first, however. What did they teach you at that wizarding school?" The sea-dragon huffed, involuntarily. The smell of sea foam and ocean currents coasted out over the white sands and up the wild grasses to the perch the young mage straddled. "As to failure, well, when you are as old as I am, you'll learn that failure is like falling out of bed — it teaches you not to sleep so close to the edge."

"You sound like my old teacher. There's no such thing as failure, he used to say, there's only — "

"Sea bass. I think I heard him say the same thing, too. Aren't we lucky to have run in the same circles."

"I remember him saying something else."

"You must have been dining on dry land."

The young mage stared out at the shoreline. The sea-dragon's tail, as imposing as a massively consequential eel, trailed out past the water's edge. The outsized tailfin fluttered occasionally, as though fanning the incoming tide. He hadn't realized how much breathing room his conjuring would take up, how monstrously substantial the thing would be. What could he have been thinking? He had wanted someone to talk to, someone to help him figure out how everything had gone wrong.

"How is Master Uzüme?"

"You know my former teacher?"

"Let's just say we've crossed paths a time or two."

"You said you ate wizards."

"Only the ones I don't like." The sea-dragon seemed to recollect something. "And he made me laugh."

The young mage scratched at an afternoon beard. "You can laugh?" His studies hadn't mentioned anything about the sense

52

of humor of legendary beasts.

"Under certain circumstances. How is he?"

"He's retired, last I heard. Moved to the Santa Clarita Valley to cultivate roses, roses without thorns. Hot, dry summer months and the occasional freezing winter — he likes his specimens hearty."

"Santa Clarita!" The sea-dragon's shoulders quavered like a mountainside about to collapse; it reared, its nostrils flaring, and snorted, the subsequent squall scattering across the horizon. The young mage held on to the boulder beneath him to keep from being bowled over. "His riddles were startling. Why is a troll a minnow one minute and a slice of cheese the next? When is four times twelve nineteen? Priceless. An accomplished poet, too. 'Recall Paris in its drowning' — one of his best! Are you sure this isn't something he'd like to help you figure out on your own?"

The young mage thought for a moment. "No, no, he's retired."

"I wouldn't be too sure," the sea-dragon insisted. "Next time you see a rose, I'd look inside its petals for a clue."

"I think we're getting off topic."

The sea-dragon stifled a yawn. "Continue."

The young mage fidgeted. Evening was fast approaching. Soon the tide would surge, soon tidal-basin frogs would gather in eddies and pools to croak at the moon, soon migrating birds would swoop down to roost along the bluffs, chasing him off his perch.

"People assume being a wizard's easy, a few tongue-swallowing words, a sprinkle of ghee here and a dash of Etrog there and voilà — happily ever after. I should have known something was up when the King told me her name was Langley. Who names the presumptive heir to a dynasty Langley? King Ahriman Angra

53

Mainyu, something or other, with that many Roman numerals attached — that's who. Twelve generations of meticulously arranged political marriages to birth a puffing-chested saysoness, a superarogating monarchship."

"Pace yourself."

The young mage wasn't listening. "Braid my hair in gold, find me a moon-valley swan, whip me up a Prince who will love me and me alone. In time for breakfast? Wasn't it enough I reversed the hex that had turned her into a spitting stone the year before? Do you know how difficult it is to find Etrog resin in the off season to weave a proper spell?"

"Generosity doesn't begin when we'd like it to begin or end when we think it should."

"I have no idea what that means."

"Which is why someone else's mess is now yours."

"I was taught to help whenever and wherever I could." The young mage looked forlorn.

"'Be that which all can look to and nothing upon which anyone can stake a claim.' That's a direct quote by the way."

"That's what I get for sleeping through morning classes."

The sea-dragon stretched and turned over. Squirmy scaly things vaulted up out of the reef and scurried for cover.

"'If a straight line falling on two straight lines makes the interior angles on the same side less than two right angles, the two straight lines, if produced indefinitely, meet on that side on which the angles are less than the two right angles.' Volume three, paragraph five, sub-chapter one. And the paragraph before and the paragraph after. Master Uzüme would read to me sometimes when I had bouts of intermittent insomnia. Certain things stayed with me."

The young mage smiled. "He was always very thoughtful."

"He's going to pamper those roses, I just know it; they'll never learn what to do with the thorns they never had."

"Now I'm exiled," the young mage cried, remembering why he'd conjured a sea-dragon out of thin air. "Loathed, hunted wherever I go. Days are the worst. Nights I can dream of companions, former classmates, friends, mystery maidens, brave little tailors tailoring. I wake up to find myself asleep in a bog or cringing below a bridge. Might as well be a foundling. Sometimes I forget why I'm alone and wander into the nearest village, to find my face plastered everywhere. Wanted: dead or alive."

"I've been depicted with two or more heads, one for breathing fire and the other for gobbling up children, as though one could choose, should choose. Or with horns on my head, like some sort of ordinary galliwasp but bigger. One idiot drew me with the head, neck and chest of a rooster, the wings of a bat, and the tail of a lizard — try living that down to your friends. Did they do a good job capturing your likeness?"

"Most times. Including the ones with the two or more heads — either way you turned, it was me. Guess they were looking for twice the reward."

"Or they wanted to make sure they could remember you no matter which eye they used."

"I should have summoned something that made more sense," the young mage said to himself.

"A distinct possibility," the sea-dragon said.

The young mage cursed his luck. He never got anything right. He gave the sea-dragon his most depressing smile. "One day I'll realize I'm making less sense than I imagined." He sat back pensively. The sea-dragon thought to do the same, in deference to his new master, but reconsidered; the gesture would have been too clumsy, and a tad condescending, to pull off.

"I'm still unsure," the sea-dragon said, "as to why the exile. You gave Langley everything she wanted."

"Exactly!"

"Stop fretting, you're making me salivate. Start in the middle and work our way to either side."

"Shouldn't I start at the beginning?" The young mage looked confused when he should have been alarmed.

"That's what you did, and look where that's gotten me."

"What do you mean?"

"Having to sit through so much misery and woe — might as well be at my parents."

"No need to be cruel. I'm the one that's been doing most of the sitting," the young mage complained.

"Insist on being accurate and I won't be able to help you." The sea-dragon heaved a beefy sigh, like the sound of surf striking the shore, long, deep, the pitch of the long note trending downward. It closed its handsome eyes, seeming to consider. "Let's start somewhere simple: tell me how you conjured up the moon-valley swan for said Langley?"

"The usual incantation," said the young mage.

> 'Light will flood the Heavens
> Summer's night is made undone.
> Power, influence, supremacy,
> Chaos' rule has just begun.
> Old magic and new enchantments
> Deliver when runic prestidigitation's done.
> Ruin toil and trouble —
> Grown to outstrip the Sun.'"

"S T O P!" the sea-dragon bellowed and, what on a different animal would have been its withers, shuddered indignantly, as though to accentuate a point or to shake off troubling emotions. "What did they teach you at that school of yours?"

"I've lost you."

"And possibly your life in the bargain." The young mage didn't respond. "Rhyming went out with the last century; no, the century before that or the one previous. Haven't you heard of free verse? internal rhyme? complex patterning? understatement? diction? denouement?"

The young mage shook his head, mystified.

"No wonder you screwed up. An incantation is a delicate instrument; damage all or some of its unmistakable structure and anything's likely to happen."

"It worked with you, didn't it? I got you here, didn't I?"

"Add being factual to your other crimes."

"What should I have done instead?"

"Something with a little flair — and a little more contemporary. Something, for example, and you can quote me — or not, it's up to you — like this:

> *'I've taught my mind*
> *To think in rhyme*
> *Internal and free falling.*
> *Yourself, you'll learn*
> *To follow downturns*
> *In the easternmost regions of trying.*
> *Babbling & barking & baffling & burbling!'*

Or better yet:

'What's afoot –
     a'holler and a'hoot –
          A meow a cow, a care a scare
     A spell is darkling made magic.'

"But you just said ... I mean, you just – that makes no sense!" The young mage furrowed his brow.

"Doesn't have to. It just has to be effective."

"Would that have worked in my case?"

"You keep hearing what I say but missing what I mean. Those two couplets were no more than simple conjurations; nonetheless, simple is better than complex, and complex more so at all.

"I think we're both getting off track here," the young mage said. "Perhaps we should stop for a while and, I don't know, relax, have something to eat."

"I thought about that earlier, but I felt sorry for you. I thought I'd just push on."

Incautiously the young mage jumped down from his perch. He walked to the shoreline, gazing out at the breakers. The sea-dragon heard what sounded like weeping. Well, there you have it, the sea-dragon thought. I should have taken that temporary teaching position at the Wizard's College when I had the chance. The world would be a whole world better by now. The young mage squatted and scooped sand into his hands, rubbing them together as though to wash away past sins or the possibility of future error. He took a deep breath, held it, and slowly blew the air from his cheeks. He ambled back, resting his shoulder against the cliff side.

The sea-dragon eyed him warily. "Shall we continue?"

The young mage nodded. "Everything went well for a while. The Prince was happy, the swan was well fed, and Langley stopped being as salty-tongued as usual. And, then, everything fell apart."

"What day was it?"

"I'm not sure — a Wednesday, I believe. What difference does that make?"

"All kinds of people get impatient as soon as the middle of the week arrives. Time seems to stand still and the weekend feels like it's been endlessly postponed," the sea-dragon said, as though stating the obvious.

"Whatever day it was, something went terribly wrong. Langley was strolling in the Royal Gardens, the Prince lounging in his room. Bored of listening to himself think the Prince bounced into the Princess' room, hoping to be distracted, and found no one there. The moon-valley swan was in its fur-lined cage, pacing behind the pearl-studded bars, coo, coo, cooing, swan, swan, swanning. The Prince assumed it was hungry. He coaxed it out of its cage and offered it some of Langley's leftover breakfast, anchovy paste on rye bread. The moon-valley swan refused it. The Prince thought, perhaps, that it needed a slice of cheese or some ale to chase it down. He began rummaging through the serving platters next to the bed. He turned in time to see the moon-valley swan dive out a side window. It had somehow managed to rip apart the drapes — coffee-red, warm muted tones, a unicorn, a stag and a crane on a mille fleur backdrop. Beelzebub and Bacall but Langley loved those drapes. I got blamed for that too — pry open the latch and escape.

"'What did you do to with my swan,' cried Langley from the doorway. 'I saw it fling itself at the horizon from the Royal Gardens.'

"'I — I …' the Prince sputtered, shrugging with his hands. Bad move. You could clearly see a smear of anchovy paste across his fingertips.

"'You skítkarl, you smeg, you oak-stump, you don't know your ass from my tits in your hands,' Langley screeched. 'Do something!'

"He could have easily responded, 'Well, they're both round, aren't they?' but he wasn't one to think on his feet. Instead he rushed out of the room and down to the stables. He jumped onto his horse, not bothering to saddle it, and flew after the long-gone moon-valley swan." The young mage stopped, gathering himself.

"And?"

"They found him months later, the Prince, that is, decomposing, entangled in brambles, two or three meters from making his way out of the enchanted forest. Seems he'd found the swan, but lost his way home. Must have gotten hungry at some point — they found roasted moon-valley swan in his belly when they autopsied him. And pieces of gold Langley had me conjure up to braid in her hair. Guess the swan had managed to wolf them down before it flew the coop. The Royal Physician never figured out if the swan or the gold, from an ancient treasure trove in Outer Mongolia, had poisoned the Prince, and then the usual, delirium, the inability to tell east from west."

"The gold, a moon-valley swan, a Prince: everything the Princess had asked for," the sea-dragon said. "To say the entire episode's ironic, would be putting too fine a point on it?"

"Langley didn't think so. Neither did the King. I was accused of indulging too many of her whims."

"Which you did."

"We have to do something," the young mage cried.

"We?"

"Why do you think I conjured you? You've lived longer than most of us; you must have answers to questions most people haven't thought to ask."

"Yes, that's what most people would think."

"Well?"

" — over there, I thought I heard voices, your majesty." The cry of alarm came from somewhere around the cliff's bend.

"We've been discovered," the young mage bawled.

"You've been discovered," the sea-dragon corrected. "I'm simply an innocent witness to this ongoing sham."

"Please. Do something."

It opened its gargantuan maw. "Here, I'll hide you."

"Ugh! the smell," the young mage objected. "How do I know you won't chew me up and forget to spit me out when you're done?"

"Look again, I have no teeth. I strain my food through the baleen plates in my mouth, like a whale. And I never spit. Lunge and gulp, I promise. That's my usual tactic."

"I'm not sure about this," the young mage said, backing away.

"There, your majesty, I think we're getting closer."

"He's right, your majesty, I see him."

The young mage looked frantic. The sun had set and the moon and stars and the tilting planets were nowhere to be seen; he was as likely to trip on his own two feet as bump into the company of soldiers giving chase if he tried to run away. He had no time to think. "Mother, sister, father, brother," he whimpered and dashed into the cavernous chops. They clamped over him. The sea-dragon gulped. It may not have had teeth but it knew how to swallow. Its gastric juices would do the rest. The young mage had never bothered to question the timing of events, had forgotten, or never knew, having slept through one too many morning classes, and the afternoon ones, that sea-dragons can throw their voice in several directions at once, in an assortment of pitches and tones and articulated nonsense, with an accuracy of nuance the wonder of seven nations. The sea-dragon burped. A misspent youth and a misspent education, why would you want to reward that? Why allow people to give reign to their worse instincts at their own expense and that of a poor moon-valley swan? Also, never ask a stranger, especially an eons-old ocean-weary sea-dragon, to solve your problems for you; he, she, it, were likely to take matters into their own hands. Those were two of the three lessons they never taught you at wizard school. Or out in the world. Until it was too late.

The moon started to rise above the horizon. A few well-executed belly rolls later the sea-dragon slid smartly into the surf. I wonder how Master Uzüme was doing, it thought. And those roses. It would have to have a talk with them at some point, and at length. Someone was going to have to educate them about their lost thorns.

Fragments

Jared awoke with a start, his hand cupped around his cock ... but, no, that was last night's joke. Let's start over.

Jared woke up trembling. His mouth tasted bitter, razor-sharp. He closed his eyes. Sleepy ... why so insistently sleepy?

He awoke with a start. At a distance, wistful, nodding music. His bladder needed emptying. The music looped and danced, looped and danced, thought after thought following blindly. He desperately needed to make water. He kept twisting in his blankets – no, not his blankets, someone else's – and just before he thought he couldn't stand it any longer, thoughts about his bladder and water closets and blankets not his own, his brain shut off, and he was asleep again.

Awake once more, head against liquid coolness, smelling incense. He felt as if he could sleep for a thousand years, and he was thirsty now. Above him, the sloping height of ... a tent? Sleep, he needed more sleep, and water, please someone give him a glass of water. Someone broke a glass, perhaps he had, the crystal beveled and clear. Sleep, he needed to sleep ... for a thousand years, a thousand, thousand years.

Voices. In the distance? nearby? Were they talking about him? It was urgent he regain his focus, his center, his aims, but not now, please god, not now.

He felt feverish. Water, someone gave him water, and he made water, with someone's help. Cool, drifting shadows, hands, tender hands, forgiving hands, at his brow.

He was caught. In moment, a significant moment, a momentous moment, a moment's moment, and half a measure more. He laughed at that, or someone did, but only in his head.

He wanted to wake up. But not really – although he did not want to be asleep either. Asleep, awake, asleep once more. Silks and satins, water and glass, a gathering of shadows, voices, voices, voices.

He awoke submitting to another set of hands, less than tender now, no longer as forgiving. Submitting as he never had before, face pressed against liquid coolness, his body astride satin sheets, someone else's body astride him. He had heard of such heresies, had been warned against them in fact, but he had been submitting all of his life, somebody else's orders, someone else's commands. He submitted as he never had before, the figures in his head stopped their looping, his thoughts their dance, he had screamed once, he remembered screaming once, and a kind of pleading, whispers in sand, little brother, hold on, hold on little brother, hold on.

When it was over, fantasy, nightmare, wish, dream, he would have to remember that voice. Not the hands, or the pleading, but the voice.

∞

My first memory, if that's what we're calling it, has me standing in shadow, my left hand against the building's rise as if to keep it from falling. Dampness coats the skin like sweat on

64

the lip of a first kiss. I'm five years old, or thereabouts, wearing a white t-shirt (but what else could it be, we're talking the late 50s), in shorts (this is Puerto Rico after all), I may or may not be wearing shoes, I may or may not be barefoot, I may or may not be wearing sandals or any other kind of footwear, hard to tell, memory displays me from the knees up, looking out into the distance, a child's distance. But that can't be, can it? In memory, as in life, shouldn't one be looking outward? the world on display instead of you? The building casts the shadow. But that can't be either. At the time, Puerto Rico, the city or town or parish I lived in, wasn't known for its city-sized buildings. In any case, I'm looking out into the near distance, unnoticed, unnoticeable, circumspect, I'm not sure about what. Children's voices in that near distance, naughty, scattershot. Instructive, don't you think, that I hadn't joined in, that I refused to join in – I was definitely refusing to join in – that I'm standing back, waiting for a sign. The sign would come, will come. I just have to wait.

∞

He lies.

But mother –

Don't be impertinent.

You married him, mother.

He married me – another lie.

Mother, please.

Listen to me, listen. They all lie.

Their shit lies, their piss lies.

Their lies lie.

The ones they rehearse in private, scare themselves with, never come back from, scatter like tears. Their kisses, their caresses lie.

They part your legs in the dark like a field they would sow

65

with their vanity, riding you within a whisper of death, listening to you whimper and wail, suppurate and fester, dribbling inside you disconsolately, teeth hard at the nipple. Like a nag they ride you at night, and wonder, oh how they wonder, why you've turned into one come daylight.

Mother!

Marry for advantage, it's what the world expects – everything else is a lie. Marry for advantage, and then take it. Beauty like yours is a waste unless it can be honed like a knife.

Men and their stinking baby-making short-swords – your father named his Lighting. *Lightning!* Claimed it never struck the same place twice! – it couldn't even find a decent cloud from which to strike much less honest ground on which to land – and it's you, you, that has to crack open, that has to yield, and they punish you for the yielding, and when you're used up they throw you away like yesterday's mutton, greedy for new meat, table scraps with their initials carved into them, you're not a woman, not a queen, not a king's daughter but a semen hamper, a broodmare, a cockloft, scions, spinoffs, issue, broods, that's all they want, putrid seed to sow more of their kind, kill them, baby girl, smother them in the birth canal if they're daughters, yes, yes, if they're daughters, throw them out into the streets before they learn to crawl, and if you can't, don't let them cry or atone, importune or supplicate, teach them to be men with slits down the middle.

Listen to me, girl-child, listen.

They'll grab at your breasts and call it an accolade, they'll drink all night with their counts and earls and palm-kissers and steal into your room and piss in the corner, clean themselves on your linens and expect you to ignore their stench, and then they'll bungle their foul-smelling cod up into you like a child contemplating his first stab at a slab of venison, apprehensive, looking at you for approval, hoping the cunt into which they hide their fears and apprehensions is heaven's bright promise or a fall into wisdom, and finished they'll skulk off only to come back later with the stink of the chambermaid or your sister or some Lady-in-Waiting on their breath and mount you, crying like yours is the first snatch they've slid into, and gash-stained, tear-stained, slobbering I'm sorry, oh, so horribly, horribly, sorry, they'll expect you to pat away their terrors and premonitions. Don't lie to yourself girl-child, don't ever lie to yourself, and if you do, if you must, if all choice has been choked and throttled from you, understand whereof and why.

Are you listening, girl-child, are you listening to me?

∞

Franklin. I'll begin with Franklin.

I met him at the gym I'd been going to. I'd come back after vacation, and he'd just joined. It wasn't love at first sight. Nothing like that.

He was not what you would call conventionally good-looking. But he wore exquisitely tailored three-piece suits and no underwear. And on the equipment he'd just used there would be the trace of some mischievous spice.

We spent the first couple of weeks eyeing each other. On the gym floor, while we exercised, in the locker room, dressing and undressing, in the sauna, drenched in bright sweat.

After a workout, he would shower, put on a pair of black socks and sit there for a few seconds as if contemplating what to do next, forgetting for the moment (not really) that he was in public view. He would play with his hair for what seemed like an eternity, and suddenly look up, remembering where he was. I often wondered what he would feel like, body glistening from

67

a shower, naked but for those black socks.

I said hello. He gave me a slight nod.

Would you spot me?

I wanted to believe he had picked me for the obvious reason, not just because I was the only person near the bench press.

How much are you pressing?

Two ten, he said.

I smiled, impressed.

I tried to say something but became conscious of the room.

That's it, he said and walked away.

He never did ask again for my help. What with summer coming on, the gym was more and more crowded. We were usually at opposite ends of the room.

He always did say hello, however. I would be concentrating on what I was doing and he'd toss me a "How's it going?" as he crossed the room.

How are you? I'd say.

But he was already past me.

Finally, there he was, in the parking lot in back of the gym. Playing with his hair, pretending he was the only one in the place. He seemed to be waiting for someone other than me.

He looked up as I walked past, reached out, and grabbed my hand.

∞

–They're everywhere nowadays.

–Who?

–Are you blind?

The two-wheeler had fallen atop the young man, legs and feet twisted painfully underneath him, one arm tucked protectively against his midsection, the other raised at an angle like an errant salute. One of the wheels was still spinning. His pants

68

were ragged and his beard stubby; the small naked lips smiled at no one – seemingly dead, except for the shallow breathing. Passersby signed apprehensions over him: "*Blessed be, blessed be.*"

– Seems to have grown right out of the pavement.

– Someone should take him home and clean him up.

– You'd have to feed him.

– Been misplaced, that's all.

– The Wardens ...

– Fit a rifle to that hand ...

– Or the Celebrants –

– Would put it to good use, wouldn't they?

– And they wouldn't have to wake him.

Signed apprehensions over him and moved on.

∞

The sound of a dog barking can be heard occasionally, but that could be an echo of an echo, yap and ricochet, it's that kind of neighborhood, posters inviting everyone to "Be a good neighbor: curb your dog" scattered usefully up and down the quiet street. It's Josh, her French bulldog, "a clown in the cloak of a philosopher," the neighbors report barking from time to time, although how that could be (rarely leaves her side, hard of hearing, nearly her age in dog years) would have surprised Caroline. He was discovered, not quite lost, not quite misplaced, by a toddler unafraid of strange-looking animals in the vicinity. His mother took the poor thing home and adopted it after negligible attempts to notify the neighborhood shelter of a possible stray. He was renamed "Who-Boy" by the toddler, presumably recalling the first few minutes they, dog and woman, that is, were introduced ("Who are you boy? Who do you belong to? Tell momma prettykins, I promise not to get mad. Tell me now,

69

who'd you run away from, huh? Who, boy, who?"), and went on to live five more years, as content as any dog his age had the wherewithal or likelihood to expect.

∞

I couldn't, I couldn't go to his funeral. He'd asked me, a week before, not to come visit him in the hospital. He couldn't stand the look in my eyes; it said more than his doctors could or dared to.

We went everywhere together. Did drag together (nearly broke an ankle the first time). Taught me to apply eyeliner to the bottom inside of my eyelids, seamlessly, imperceptibly, to give them depth. Convinced me contact-lenses were a much better look for me than the fashionable glasses I always wore. Coached me in loosening up. Encouraged me not to quote Rimbaud (or Joyce or Eliot) to guys who only wanted to get inside my pants. Barbara Streisand. Barbara Streisand. Barbara Streisand.

There he is as Cat Woman. And there again as a Martian princess. There he is as this year's runner-up Miss America, a reluctant bride-to-be, Sacajawea, Indian maiden, and Mother Superior Jumped the Gun (you had to be there). And there again in a skirt made of foam rubber shaped into legs, heels and all, nylons and all, the Rockettes would have been proud of. At a distance you couldn't tell if he had crossed his legs or they had, at their own insistence.

Jesus, Dana, if you're going to wear heels, learn to dance in them like you mean it. You look like a man in drag.

I *am* a man in drag.

I know, I know. But it's not a pastime, it's a tradition.

Rene Saucedo, best friend, 33 years of age, 1986, dead of complications from AIDS. The month escapes me. The day escapes me.

Once, not long afterwards, I dreamed that I was in heaven, and there he was in that red shirt he had lent me more than once.

What the hell are you doing here? he said, a little troubled, a little piqued.

What do you mean? Where else am I supposed to be?

Look, I know the shopping's great and all that but it's not your time. He shushed me away. I hesitated. Go, he said, go.

∞

A dog barked, another dog answered.

– We live in a society –

– Obviously.

– My mother thought –

– And yet you survived childhood, didn't you?

– It's invective, sheer spite …

– But under the right circumstances, it works, doesn't it?

– You can't really believe that?

– Dystopia, don't you see, had to be invented so that we could have something to talk about.

– What other crap are they feeding you? Filthy academics.

– Marry me.

– Sure, why not?

– Suffering is no stranger to life … and life no stranger to suffering.

– Keep writing stuff like that and no one will publish it.

– The Firebird Sonata in C minor, I believe.

– I thought he'd died years ago.

– Before he died … he composed it hours before he died.

– The calculation for density of space starts by counting the N allowed states at a certain k that are contained $[k, k+dk]$ inside the volume of the system. This is done by differentiating the whole k-space volume in n-dimensions at an arbitrary k, with respect to k. The volume, area or length in 3, 2 or 1-dimensional spherical k-spaces are then expressed by –

– Filthy academics.

– How are the kids?

– Like everyone else's, they're out pretending they're well-behaved.

– On the other hand.

– That makes four exceptions – how many hands do you have?

∞

Simi Valley is a smallish bedroom community on the outskirts of the San Fernando Valley. Houses, flat and one-dimensional, face one another across streets with little or no sidewalk. Even the vistas are flat, so that the eye, seeking the horizon, gets stuck in the middle distance. Yet here and there tall and ethereal-looking palm trees reach majestically toward the sky, colonial in their splendor. Hometown, U.S.A., California-style.

A humdrum social redoubt tucked sleepily against flowering foothills and the beginnings of sparse forestland, it is less planned community than an accretion of buildings. What passes for its main street crisscrosses the town, feeding into the highway at one end, at the other disappearing past quaint neighborhoods into treacherous hills. At its center administrative buildings part Greek revival part modernist ambition command rightful derision. Yet, if truth be told, the corridors are generous, with offices welcoming and designed for the business at hand. Coyotes and the rare mountain lion roam meanderingly through side streets and alleys. Otherwise the most dangerous things wandering about are octogenarians way beyond driving age. Simi Valley has the highest concentration of police officers living within the bounds of the city and a well-earned reputation for being the safest piece of real estate in what is known as the Greater Los Angeles Metropolitan Area. Who would have thought he'd go missing?

"They're saying they found a set of bones out in the woods," said Mrs. Myers, always the bearer of bad news. "They'd been picked clean, and white as a salt lick, like the bones of a saint. They're going to run those test they do nowadays to try and figure out if it's the Evans boy."

Mr. Myers, noting the look on my face, tried to interfere. "Gladys, I don't think a body can decompose so quickly in such a short time – it's only been a few weeks."

"Oh, what do you know," shouting now, even though she was the one who was deaf. "He was such a tiny thing for his age, anything's possible." And headed off towards the dairy isle. Mr. Myers rushed after her.

∞

Well?

words

intermediaries

the spaces between

You should have thought of that when you set the whole thing in motion, he said.

One of the points of light detached itself from the swarm and advanced toward him. Hudson fell to his knees, head swimming with phantasmagoria, dream. The images were like his visions, always in the third person, a narrative run asking to be read out loud so that the ear registering the sounds, comedy, tragedy, burlesque, would understand they were supposed to mean something. He had been chosen, used, something akin

73

to a last judgment, because the possibility of that judgment needed flesh and its motives to understand an irrevocable verdict could not be abstracted from the worldly facts that gave it meaning. The first of these facts had him as a hollow starving thing in a child's body, the bottom of his feet bleeding from the jagged rocks he'd run across to get as far as he could, for as long as he could. He had almost succeeded. The outcropping looked out over a gorge. There was a river down there, running lazy turns around hills jutting up, up, up to the skyline. The rocks beneath his feet were slick with blood; brutal footprints ran toward him from a distance, as though something chased him, and would yet catch up. He stepped off. The blast of air hit him and he had tumbled freely, but only for a moment. In the next he was soaring, past hills and rises, the turquoise skyline, caught up in his own mystery. He would never to be allowed to step off. He had a verdict to deliver, a last judgment, but not yet, the life he was supposed to have lived, that had lived him, through him and as him, was now a thing deferred, if not forever for the distant future.

Are you alright? Paderborn, at his side, helping him up.

I was a boy once, he said.

∞

– Hey there.

?

– Are you all right?

?

– You can't sleep there you know.

– Wasn't.

– Wasn't what?

– Asleep.

– Then what?

74

– Dead.

!

–The dead don't dream and I wasn't dreaming ... so dead.

– I don't dream.

–Then you're dead too.

– Look, you can't be.

–Why not?

– Because you're talking to me. ...

–The dead don't talk? What kind of nonsense is that?

– Look –

– How do I know you're not dead?

– Because I'm not ... just like I know you're alive and talking to me and not dreaming.

– But that's what I said – so dead.

– Now see here, we'll have to call the police.

– How do I know they're not dead, too?

– Bitterness is a poison that eats at the soul. 'Bury the dead,' the ancients say, 'and let them stay buried.' Resentment is a curse.

–That's a joke, right? Tell me that's a joke?

∞

It is a small clamorous town, big city, city-town, big and small, the overlapping features of which make for interesting conversation, somewhere in the Midwest perhaps, the Southwest possibly, Up North or the South out of the question, let's not quarrel over motive or reason, not now or in the near future. The West then, if we must, let's call it the West: several strains of ash, several more of oak and pine, the beguiling sunlight, the wonder of endless, echoing waves, the desert calm. At the water's edge, his face, what you could see of it beneath the silly hat, had a kind of biblical cast, something to do with the way he tilted his head when listening to you. Rather, when he wasn't listening to you, listening to anyone. Noah's silence. He was listening for that. Or perhaps he was listening for his own.

What are you going to do now?

I can't very well dig her up to prove a point, can I? Not if I don't know where she's buried.

We could ask. Officially and otherwise.

I think we're beyond that.

He closed his eyes, as though he would sleep, right here, right now, as though he could sleep. I stared out at he waves, the horizon, stared out for him, gauging the distance. He was going to need a witness, someone needed a witness. I suppose that's why I came out here with him. Would they believe him now? would they ever believe him?

∞

Where to start? al-Kindi's brief but excellent *R. fi'l-Jirm al-Hamil bi-Tiba'ihi al-Lawn min al-anasir al-Arba'a wa alladhi-huwa 'Illa al-Lawn fiGhayrihi*, Abu Rida, vol. II, 64-8? Or time's arrow, luck and happenstance (see J. Janssens, "al-Kindi's Concept of God," Ultimate Reality and Meaning 17 1994:7)? Better yet: the so-called *Sæm'a-el* ('Blind God') Fragment, which scholars would have us believe is part of the larger *Trimorphic Protennoia*.

Blind I gambled, blind I stumbled, a million alternatives plus one. Fragmentum B1.

We have memories of the past, not of the future. Think fast: which should have priority over the other? Fragmentum B4a.

The moving now, earlier, later than, presence and subsistence, all have a function, not to be lauded as man-made because we've had a hand in their perfection. Fragmentum 12.

Fact after fact: look at the net and not at what it traps. Fragmentum 16.

Bid me a gopher and ride its back as far as the waters take you. Fragmentum 17 (disputed).

The world begets and destroys in her own fashion. Beware not the garment but she who would stoop to wear it. Fragmentum 19.

There once will have been a current, there once will have been a shore. Tell me oh bright one on whose authority do you believe the shaping is done. Fragmentum 21 (reconstructed).

Brood Hen has an incomparable killing talent; no, no talent whatsoever: both metaphysical truisms if one knows how to debate which is which in connection to the matter at hand. Fragmentum 25.

Behold: who but the people can travel two hundred and forty miles to stand still and, standing still, be. Fragmentum 32 (possibly corrupt).

Time: a delicacy local reckoning rarely takes notice of but that history calls War and Change. Lost Fragment (also possibly corrupted).

God, man, the universe: all equal parts and half the equation. Equal for equals, unequal for unequals, different for different levels, the same for same domains, the lawful thing not by accident the just. – *Trimorphic Protennoia*, V.19.1248c14-15.

And to be fair:

The point of morality is to make moral distinctions; the point of government is to govern. The difference is categorical. What would you say if the terms under discussion were religion and its counterpart? – *The Disjunctive Heresy*, Minakanushi-no-kami.

∞

I follow my friend outside. It's nighttime. I feel a sudden rush of alarm and struggle to swallow it down. It's nothing. I've felt it before, a sudden quickening, adrenaline in the system, panic on the tongue. Earlier today, wasn't it? In any case, plenty of times. It always comes up with such a start. I stop, look around as though for a warning from the surrounding landscape – but there's only the surrounding landscape. It's probably an animal thing, deposited in the blood eons ago, biding its time to come up just so, a trick of the genes rather than destiny.

"Are you coming?" My friend tugs at my sleeve.

"No. I'm going to stand here and pretend I'm a tree."

"Come on."

I start to walk faster. The quickening is in my footsteps now, where I can keep up with it, keep it under control. An animal thing, after all.

Better that than to admit to myself that lately I'm frightened much of the time. The other day I was sitting in front of the TV watching a 42 year-old man telling the world that he'd been a child-molester since adolescence, that he'd be one still had he not been caught. The camera had zoomed in for a close up, seeking his face, seeking a truth behind this big, monstrous se-cret. He'd looked up and smiled at it with a kind of childlike glee. He spoke without guile, without much regret, baring his soul with open-eyed wonder – not to the interviewer, the stranger who'd come to collect the sad facts of his life, but to the camera, the eye of millions, with the kind of intimacy with which he'd step into his bath or turn on his television and feel once more the first faint flicker of life, pulsating, electronic, "live." Looking in on someone else's life, participating in someone else's se-cret, I felt as if I were being watched, as if I were being judged.

Friends of mine were robbed at gun point as they'd been getting ready for dinner. The robbers had pried open a bedroom window and crawled in. Suddenly, there they were, between the rattle of dishes and the boiling vegetables.

The night air is crisp, bracing, indifferent. I move quickly but carefully, afraid to bump into the sharp edge of things.

The young man on the witness stand smiled earnestly, a kid in a spelling bee sure he would win. It was a documentary on skinheads. He was describing the number of blows it took to crush in a man's skull, the purpling flesh, the sound of bone breaking, brain matter on the pavement, the blood on the baseball bat that wouldn't rub off no matter how many times he'd wiped it clean. That the man he'd clubbed to death had been a human being minutes before the rain of deadly blows was a distant concern to him, the dead man a statistic (he'd done this before), an abstraction, what everyone and everything outside his tight circle of friends and ideology was to him anyway. But damn it if he couldn't get the blood on the bat to wash off.

I grab at my friend's shoulder. "What's the hurry – the car's only a few blocks away."

"I don't relish being the only ones out here by ourselves. This isn't exactly friendly territory."

As if that mattered. On a street like this one, in the middle of a city that bills itself as the "Gayest City This Side of San Francisco," a carload of teenagers from the other side of town, yelling "Die faggots, die!", had showered birdshot at a group of passersby. On another night, in a nearby park, two men wearing ski masks had jumped a young man using the park as a short cut. They'd yelled the word "Queer!" over and over again as the young man cried out in pain. Screams of help had brought a woman from somewhere in the dark. "Stop it! Stop it now!"

79

she'd shouted. The two men had thrown her to the ground. One of them slapped her hard, bringing blood to her mouth. They'd run away laughing.

∞

The Sea-of-Translation was just around the corner. Novice-In-Training Pema Zöet could hear it, crest upon deafening crest crashing against the irregularly toothed ridge of sandstone reaching down its enormous height to caress its jawline against the Sea and guide it headlong into a body of water twice its size. Enumclaw Major was somewhere up there atop Conglomerate Stalwart, chief among this particular collection of sea-stacks separating coastline from headland, up there laughing at their struggle to keep feet and hands from slipping out from underneath them as they inched their way up the bluff's rise. Some had lost the fight and fallen to an early death or some state close enough. You'd think Enumclaw Major would throw down a rope or an anchor line, anything that would help. Group strength, group solidarity, wasn't that the point of the exercise, up, up, up, foot grip to handhold, cliff side to rockface, with as much left in reserve to sprint to the finish line, a test of mettle not a collective maiming or communal suicide. That wasn't going to happen. Enumclaw Major had to prove she was better than the other Preceptors. The Novices-In-Training assigned to her had to be the best, had to learn that no enterprise was worth pursuing if the possibility of death wasn't a measure of that endeavor.

Novice-In-Training Pema Zöet continued his climb. He would not shame himself, would not shame First-Father and Concubine-First-Mother or the rest of his brothersisters/sisterbrothers. He just had to remember not to look down. Down was death and damnation. He meant to postpone both as long as he could, long after his kill-ratio had increased to the point where he would be granted Dominant-Rank. One day he too would be First-Father, one day he too would combine seed to egg, one day he and his Concubine-First-Mother would fetch First-Born from Placentæ-Prime where they had been authorized to develop from embed to blastocyst to womb-child to initiate herhim/himher to the time-worn, time-tested traditions of nation and state, one day his First-Born would be a Novice-In-Training, enrolled here at Kilkenny GraveBar in fact, striving against their own Enumclaw Major, determined to make kith and kin proud. Novice-In-Training Pema Zöet took a deep breath and continued. First-Borns never gave up. He just had to push himself, translating indoor skills into outdoor movement. Clip and go, as he'd been trained to do. Cover as much ground as possible, letting instinct born out of that deep training dictate what hand went up first, what foot last, momentum taking up the slack. Five pitches, max 7a, 6b+ obl and S1 bolting, overhangs all along the way. Nothing but the best, most dangerous climbs for Enumclaw Major's Novices-In-Training.

Novice-In-Training Pema Zöet was already high enough so that the sea breeze no longer made the rockface slippery. Go, he told himself, move, goddamn it, move. It wasn't just a matter of finishing first. This was a timed test. He could reach the finish line before the rest of the troop and still fail. There was a sudden squeal down and to his left, a no-nonsense yelp that never reached its sharp unsuspecting endnote. Gusts of wind whipped the sound up across the rockface, where it bounced to strike at elbows and knees, and nearly knocked him offstride. He wouldn't, he couldn't look, move, goddam it, move. A few meters more and he would be up and over. First-Borns never lost.

81

∞

Should I tell you how we were anticipated, out-maneuvered, outthought, out-gunned?

Should I tell you that fate has a perverse sense of humor, polymorphously perverse, that it teases and clowns as an errant child?

Should I speak of hubris, of language and its abstractions, of goals and objectives as poor as they are bone dry?

Should I?

No One Reads Hemingway Anymore

The blue expanse. The cresting waves. The endless coastline. The clouds, the sky, the blue within blue within blue. The lone sailboat, the sun, the surf, the sand. Around every turn, every bend, every opportunity, cheap sentiment yours for the asking. With every incline, slight pitch or sudden slant, there it is. And there again. Keep your eyes on the road, Marvin, keep your eyes on the road.

Clouds intermittently obscure an oblate sun, marine shoreline reflecting marine skyline. On the other side, obstinate hillsides. Out here, they're called mountains. But if you've crisscrossed the Alleghenies or skirted the Sierras, as he has, you've earned the right to call them rank amateurs, pigmy crags and struggling shrub stripped of wild life. On the radio, someone is wailing. *"We are stardust, we are golden ... and we got to get ourselves back to the G A – A – AHH RDEN!"* Thank God, the windows are up.

That morning on the second day of a long holiday weekend, he'd decided to head up the coastline and found himself on his way to Ventura County, the City of Buenaventura. Perhaps he'll peek into the antique stores, idle at the used-book stores, wander into the girly shops, the thrift stores, the sandalwood-and-soap boutiques, contemplate the special sampler, dark ale to light beer, at the storefront brewery on Main Street, savor the tri-tip for which the county is known, hazard a Tarot card reading from the undernourished kid behind the counter, nose ring, piercings, body implants, surely he'd know something about fate and destiny. Cloud-blessed City of San Buenaventura. Too many tattoos and too many navels, too many recently married couples and too many bouncing babies, the surprise of overweight Lesbians in Bermuda shorts who thought they owned the sidewalk, the aging surfers with meager breastbones and airless bottoms in skintight wetsuits riding wave after wave into the sunset, the occasional Northern European visitor turning up at every corner: someone must have told them of the bargain antiques and the welcoming salt-sea air.

Canna had refused to come with him, something about visiting friends, something she'd scheduled awhile back. First there would have been Camus ("Hegel, of course, permits the forgiveness of sins at the end of history. Until then, however, every human activity is sinful."), then Dylan ("I set my monkey on the log, and ordered him to do the Dog. He wagged his tail and shook his head, and he went and did the Cat instead."), something from the metaphysical poets ("My bent thoughts, like a brittle bow, / Did fly asunder: / Each took his way; some would to pleasures go, / Some to the wars and thunder."), with a backswing at Hendrix ("You have to forget about what other people say, when you're supposed to die, or when you're supposed to

84

be loving. You have to forget about all these things."). It wasn't the quotes themselves she minded, late in the afternoon, before or after sex, especially the fun and teasing ones, and if he was pretending to say something. It was the sudden hard and fast and mournful leaps across the gap, the sharp veering to one side or the other without bothering to determine if the back and forth was being done under the right circumstances, the right scope or breadth of meaning. Better he go off on his own, take the weekend to wind down, do a bit of soul searching. Or it could simply be she wanted to visit her friends. So here he is out on his own, yet again some would say, and eager for blood; but, really, he simply wants to stretch his bones, play out the crick in his neck, crack a knuckle or two. He's fixed as much as he's willing to fix around the house, and he's been meaning to get to this month's American Classics recommendation, Sandburg's *Abraham Lincoln, The Prairie Years and The War Years* (the Definitive One-Volume Edition). There's the black and white portrait of the great man on the cover, slightly walleyed, the left one from the look of it, the great historical miracle, and a wonderfully terse blurb, a kind of gloss actually, there above the title. Then of course, there's Sandburg. Sandburg's Lincoln.

Past Point Hueneme the road turns inward along a stretch of agricultural fields profligate in their splendor and trails off through the squalor of downtown Oxnard. Dusty shops on dusty streets, the lone storekeeper looking off at the distance, nodding off now and then, dreaming of customers that whizz by, carloads of them, on their way to the outlet mall farther inland (he would weep but what would be the point; he should have sold out when he had a chance). To be followed by recent development, so much glass bounded by so much masonry, buff, olive, mushroom, fawn, the approach curving and tiled or straightforward and paved, the overhang faux lintel or naked joists.

Judy in disguise, well that's a-what you are
a-lemonade pies, with a brand new car
cantaloupe eyes come to me tonight
you're Judy in disguise, with glasses

keep a-wearing your bracelets, and your new rah rah
a-cross your heart, yeah, with your living bra
a-chimney sweep sparrow with guys
you're Judy in disguise, with glasses

Marvin and his wife live in what was once a minor artist community — of minor artists; communist cells secreted revolutionary aspirations there throughout the 50s; the 70s spawned disenchanted youth angling for the cheap rents and pockets of green the place affords; the homosexual community followed; now the rock-and-roll set, or whatever they're called these days, are settling into the place. Man-made or not, it's the glistening lake that attracts them and, despite suicidal curves, the steep ambition of the streets.

One of his neighbors owns a cat with the territorial instincts of a Nazi. He keeps a lovely little beastly finch in a plumy brown blazer with an agreeable yellow stripe like a tie down its feathery breast. A society finch, a bird in a suit, his Blake. Seven notes to its song, which it strings three-four three-four three-four up the scale until the repeat finds its freedom and escapes the room. The tiny thing cleaves zealously to its perch even after he opens the door to its cage, offering it a bit of self-determination now and then. He's starting to believe Blake finds his actions somewhat suspect — the modern temper. Nonetheless, he feeds and changes its water every day and discourages the neighbor's cat with a few rounds from a grease gun. The neighbor's floors must be an oily tapestry by now, she should teach it not to wander.

Another neighbor plays his stereo (Pup, Wild Nothing, Chairlift) late into the evening, late late into the night. Marvin's called the police several times but it didn't help. The neighbor's house is bounded by strangling bushes, a monumental oak or two, flowerbeds without flowers, a redundancy of vines and an ivy-bound trellis permanently on the mend. A putto without a fountain, he frolics through the backyard garden semi-nude late into the night when he thinks no one's looking.

Last week Marvin spotted him scurrying out the front door, leaving it unlocked. He'd jumped into his car and skidded off, showering the neighborhood kids with loose gravel. What a fool! One of these days he'll come back to find everything in his house fingered and poked through. The ransacked house would be a clear judgment, a sense that you can't always have your way in the world. I should teach him a lesson, Marvin thought. It would be simple. From his side door, it would be but a few steps to a cut in the bushes. He would have to hurry. Start with the stereo, a sole kick and it would topple, the large-screen television cracked to blindness, the bookshelf slapped of its Books-of-the-Month, the bric-a-brac clubbed to the floor, a kitchen knife to the garage-sale furniture, the stuffing scattered everywhere like alien spoor, the kitchen cabinets gutted, the oranges and bananas on the counter choked of their pulp and spanked against the walls like obscene graffiti, the dresser bureau sacked, moth-eaten underwear and dirty socks carpeting the floor like soiled snow, the single bed in the bedroom (who'd

87

have the courage to sleep with him?) plundered and pissed on, the stream hissing on the coverlet like an epithet, bathroom towels strangling the shower head like clown bowties, floor mats stuffed into the toilet bowl, the water running and surging and spilling everywhere. What else? The windows, take a brick to the windows, gouge and smash and shatter, maim and maul, butcher everything. He'd have to change into a pair of boots and a pair of gloves. Did he own a pair of gloves? But his neighbor had rounded the corner in no time, the backseat crammed with groceries. He could have done it, damn him, he could have! Oh, well, better that it had come to nothing. He hated that lately his response to everything was an emotional one.

Across the street, someone had converted the ramshackle ranch-style house into a meeting place for twelve-steppers. It has a long low profile and curtainless windows. One day at a time, one day at a time. Once a man with hair the color of wheat came out and glanced from one corner of the street to the other. Loose-limbed, long-necked, still young, still thinking in paradox. He tapped a long yellow pencil against his teeth; someone must have given him a quota. He waved at Marvin and dived back inside the house. Marvin startled himself by waving back.

Mr. Lee, of *Mr. Lee's Fruits & Veg'tables*, the local mom-and-pop down on Hyperion, was for all intents and purposes an incorrigible Chinese coolie (his forbears had been in America since the 1800s, and were all naturalized). He spoke an improbable pidgin, or some such cousin, solicitous, smiling and bowing and scraping, "'Alo, 'alo, you wanting milk today?" He was short and slightly bowlegged, what the stereotype called for. "No carrots, no carrots, Tuesday or Sunday, plenty, plenty." Marvin imagined he had been called for the role and had come running. Marvin imagined he was trying to fit in.

88

"Mr. Lee?"

"Yes, yes," from across the counter.

"You promised me winter peaches."

"Yes, yes, promise, promise, yes, yes," smiling interminably, head bobbing as though his neck muscles were on a spring. "Persimmons, pomegranates, tangerines, plenty favorite, everybody buy."

He imagined him as another cliché: Mr. Lee at home in a smoking jacket reading Waugh or Maugham to his mastiff and sundry relations in the comforts of his wood-framed, wood-paneled reading room. Somehow, somewhere, some ambition had gone awry.

"See you Thursday Mr. Lee."

"Yes, yes. Yes, yes."

There was a famous Mexican restaurant farther down the street, waiters and servers colorfully dressed, a gay sex club that opened Sundays sunrise to sunset, you could skip Church, and a bookstore with out-of-prints and a bargain basement.

Hello, I love you
Won't you tell me your name?
Hello, I love you
Let me jump in your game
Hello, I love you
Won't you tell me your name?
Hello, I love you

A delayed moon, the night cold and dark as a tunnel. Generally he would pretend to close his eyes and fall asleep and dream a little, his head at rest atop the half wall at the window, the lake across and below him glimmering and silver, whispering its tale to the concrete and the fencing that surrounds it. He worried it would not be heard, worried it would not be understood. This late at night someone would be walking his dog, someone would be on the swing in the park legs up up in the air in adult spectacle and wonder. A giggle or two, raucous and bawdy, but she would not stop. Nor would he want her to. The world was awfully quiet. He began whispering to himself. The messenger never rests until the message is delivered. He doesn't know what that means. Who'd be knocking at his door this late at night? Was he pitching in his sleep? Wasn't everybody unhappy in his or her own way? But then he'd be broadsided by the scent of soap on freshly laundered skin and turn in time to glimpse a brightly colored skirt flouncing in the breeze and would think, how, how could she be unhappy, smelling and looking like that. Kissing her, he knew, would be like biting into a peach, downy and sweet, the stubble on his chin provoking a smile and the want of another kiss, even if from middle-aged lips. He wanted to believe in pathos, but that was just a word in a book, a word no one bothered to look up or use in real life. What if someone could reach in, his wife perhaps, the guy next door, Phanindra at the corner 7Eleven, Aracelio at the neighborhood gas station, grab at his heart and give it a good, stiff shake, until all the shit fell away? What a joke. Were all men his age as conceited, he wondered, as touchingly maudlin, in their going concerns?

That Tuesday, or the one before that, or the one after, he wasn't always sure, his brother called.

"Marv."

"Jess."

"How are you doing?"

"I'm fine — why'd you ask?"

"So you'd ask back, you dumb fuck. I'm your brother."

"All right, all right. How are *you* doing?"

"Like Samson, I'm in the dark, and continue to ride the bus."

He was quoting someone, he was always quoting someone. They were brothers, weren't they?

"Did you get to where you wanted? Or was it an Express and you missed your stop?"

"That's what I love about you, Marv, we all do, you always know how to play the game."

Not always. The other evening someone had knocked on his door, flourished a petition and demanded a contribution. "I'm from Common Cause," the young girl said. "Which one?" Marvin said. He slammed the door on her handsome face.

"Well?"

"We're not moving to Phoenix, Jess."

"You could start over."

"Why would I want to do that?"

"You've got hidden talents, Marv. I'm good with a pick and shovel. I could help you dig them up."

He thought of his brother's rather heroic ankles.

"You could be so many things here," his brother went on. "A consulting apprentice, a body donation courier, a make-it-in-Germany recruiter, a Thomist-in-hiding, a promoter of the higher diction, a tenure-track faculty fellow in mysticism and the hidden realms, an administrator of big data, a principal and principled investigator of the hologram, virtuoso in computational biology, groundbreaker in genomic stratification (patient-focused), are you starting to detect a trend?, advance man of mindsets and counterfactuals, the driving force in neurodegenerative disorders, postdoc in the pathogenesis of mosquito-borne diseases, finalist in the Alexander von Homboldt professorship sweepstakes, Phoenix gets more and more interesting by the minute, doesn't it Marv? Perhaps all of Arizona? Perhaps all of the Southwest?"

"I thought Phoenix was where snowbirds from Calgary or Minnesota go to play golf."

"And think big thoughts, Marv. How better to envision the next turn in stochastics than in 115 degree weather?"

"Why are you telling me this?"

"You're the smart one, Marv, you know things, many things. How smoke coils in on itself counter-clockwise when no one's looking? when butter was invented? what line of dialogue ended Keaton's career? how many Japanese particles have prepositional attributes? why cats dream of segmented crustaceans? why Cather is a more important writer than Barnes? and not just for Nebraskans? Phoenix needs you, Marv, I need you, god's country needs you. We have no major libraries or museums I can think of, and if we do both are closed for permanent repairs."

Marvin laughed. "Can I bring my books? All of them?"

"You can bring Canna if you insist. But she's under your watch and care. Don't forget, we're steak and potatoes country here."

"I don't know, I just ..."

"What makes the Hottentot so hot? What puts the 'ape' in apricot? What have they got that you ain't got?"

"Really, Jess? Really?"

"So decide already."

"Next Tuesday of next year. Or the year next. I'll decide. I swear."

"You could move in phases."

"I'll decide, I'll decide."

"But none of the usual shenanigans."

Of all his family, he loves his brother best. Why has he never bothered to tell him?

"Call me, okay."

"I thought I just did."

"That was me, numbskull. Love you."

There, someone said it.

Well, I've never been to Spain
But I kinda like the music
Say the ladies are insane there
And they sure know how to use it
They don't abuse it
Never gonna lose it
I can't refuse it

"I saw a rat down by the dumpster the other day," Mrs. Fitzgerald complained. "I may be old but I'm not stupid. He said it was a field mouse — but it was a rat!"

Mrs. Fitzgerald is stooped and folded back in on herself like a pretzel; she wouldn't have had to look down to see anything scurry past her. Every Sunday she walks downhill the two or three blocks to the Presbyterian Church on the corner, a nose-gay of cherry blossoms astride the pillbox hat she always wears for the occasion. The first time they had visited her apartment, Marvin and Canna marveled at the bright trim lambrequins on every window of the place. For a while, they entertained the idea of having a pair installed in their master bedroom. They settled for rickracks with matching tiebacks instead.

"He's a fascist, that's what!" She must have seen him turning on the sprinklers in the front yard and rushed over. "A rent strike — that would teach him! He listens with his pocketbook

93

— that's where we should hit him! I've tried to tell the other tenants we should organize. But they're either too young to know better or from some country where they shoot you if you so much as dream of these things." She'd dogged him back to his front door. "You're the talker, you're the persuader, help me make history."

That had been Tuesday. By then he had been eager to get out of town, although the weekend was three days away.

Every summer, during his three months away from the classroom, he read Hemingway, top to bottom, juvenilia to just before the old man crawled into a corner and blew his head off. He wasn't sure why. Canna would let him make love to her without protest, stroking his back as though she meant it, as though they were sharing the same set of memories and the prospect of honest conversation. He would bite down on his lip for a moment, to keep his heart from breaking. Autumn would come around soon enough, the school year would begin anew, and with it, his mood swings. Canna would take to the guest bedroom. He could retire, he'd put in enough years, or find another line of work, they'd talked about it often enough.

"They're nothing but thugs," she would say. "You've put in your time; you don't owe anyone anything."

"You watch too much television Canna. It's nothing like they make it out to be," biting into, what? Kale, she had called it. Arugula, Swiss shard, mustard greens, foods that heal — they were turning into goats. "They're kids, for God's sake — testosterone on overdrive, and girls who can't figure out which end of a tampon to stick up their cooch."

"I hate it when you talk like that," starting to clear her side of the table. "It doesn't make you right or me wrong."

He should have asked her about her day, should have tried

to distract himself, the two of them. She could always tell when he'd had a bad day. So, of course, she had asked. And, of course, he had answered. He hated lying to her. Not from any scruple, mind you; he just wasn't good at it; not with her.

"Second period turned in a couple of solid C-pluses. That's at least something."

"A couple of C-pluses — in how many years?" In the kitchen now, filling up the dishwasher, storing leftovers away. "Jesus, Marvin, that kind of news wouldn't even cheer up a second-rate undertaker."

"It's something, Canna, it's something. Give me a break, will you?"

"Have it your way. I'm going to bed."

"It's something," he said, spooning goat food into his mouth.

He was sitting in the lounge of the Empire Hotel
He was drinking for diversion
He was thinking for himself
A little money riding on the Maple Leafs
Along comes a lady in lacy sleeves ...
Hey honey-you've got lots of cash
Bring us round a bottle
And we'll have some laughs
Gin's what I'm drinking
I was raised on robbery

"Who Johnson?" he said, "'Who has an idea of right, the confidence of providence or the simple prurience of an original imagination?'" It wasn't Hemingway but it would do.

Johnson stared at him, nervous a little, frightened a little, was Mr. Holman like being for real? yes, well, he might just be,

95

was he like cracking up? he just might be, why was he smiling so, like he knew something? he just might, and forgot to bark back his usual answer.

He stared back at the kid. God bless him, god bless them all; they were all waiting for a miracle to occur.

Marvin was truculent in his insistence he'd been born to teach. Marvin being Marvin in a Marvish way. Negotiating from a higher position, what some called funny business, what he called teaching, some bit of this, some bit of not, whatever the moment called for, even if it ended up in some form of bullying. "Mr. Holman, Mr. Holman, why you gotta be that way? I'll put it away, I swear. Ah, man — I mean, sir. ... That was my grandma, man, she just passed away. Like her last known text on earth. Why you think I be countering? She like by now been gone sometime why she waiting for someone to sign her back. ... Wait, wait, hold on now. ... Nah now, that's like a million miles of wrong, Mr. Holman, a million wrong. ... Okay, okay, but I want it back when class is over. That cost me a month of green." Once or twice a year, once or twice a semester if he was lucky, some punk kid in an individual sweater and a mood she could call her own would coax open a book and spend an eternity turning pages. He'd seen it, been witness to it. Once or twice. Besides, he looked forward to his three months off once a year, making believe this year, this year, he'd do something with those three months. But year in and year out there was mostly Hemingway, and the long slow untranslatable summers with Canna curled next to him, her breathing soft and nocturnal, the breeze off the lake in through the window gentle against naked flesh. He pretended he was happy, twelve plus years, what else could you ask for? He'd walk into the den in time to eavesdrop on Blake crooning in his cage. The neighbor's cat would cross

96

the street when he was in the driveway looking for nothing in particular. Even the twelve-steppers across the way looked as if God had finally granted them the wisdom to know better. He raked leaves in the small backyard, he pruned the hydrangeas in the front yard, he puttered and planned.

And would let Mrs. Fitzgerald ramble whenever she visited. "In my day people were more circumspect," she would say, emerald-green eyes not the least bit rheumy or lost. He tried to imagine her young again, garden-fresh, captive to a future she had yet to step into. She had been flirtatious in her day, earning something (experience he supposed, and what else?), something she hadn't yet figured out how to spend, if she would have to, and what the other side of that spend would be.

"It's a kind of narcissism, don't you think?"

"I'm sorry, Kathleen," using her Christian name, "I lost track there for a second."

"Always trying to get ahead of things, Marvin, betwixt. It's a marvel you get anything done in the now."

He nodded toward his garden. "Must be doing something right."

"That's not you, you fool thing, that's your hands, memory or resourcefulness, I couldn't tell you, and I bet you couldn't tell me either. For God's sake, Marvin, there's no mystery to how the body works. That's what it's supposed to do."

"You're using the Lord's name in vain again, Kathleen."

"As if you and me would know what He thinks vain. As if you care enough to care about these things."

"I have depths, Kathleen, levels, dimensions, pockets of warmth and regard. I care, Kathleen, I care."

"Care where you're aiming that thing Marvin. You nearly got my shoes. Oh, look." She picked something up. She gestured at him with it and went to sit on the lone garden bench. "My mother had the fanciest things to say about dandelions. Her heart would break to think people believe they're weeds."

He took a good look at it. "I believe that's a cat's-ear, Kathleen, what's called a false dandelion."

"How can a thing be false? Either it is or it isn't. What would this lovely thing have to falsify?"

"What I meant was — "

"I know what you meant. Such a stickler."

"What I was trying to say — "

"That's the problem Marvin, you're always trying."

"It's who I am, Kathleen, it's who I am."

"I'm nearly two hundred fifteen and I don't know who I am. Who are you to be so adamant about it?"

"You just said — "

"Oh Marvin, I know what I said."

He looked up at her from where he was kneeling. "You have the loveliest green eyes Kathleen. I bet men fought duel after duel to get within easy distance."

"Duels, Marvin, *duels*! You'd think I was two hundred fifteen."

He heard Canna calling his name from inside the house.

"Have to go," leaning in to kiss her on her cheek.

"Ever on the leash, I see."

"She's not the enemy, Kathleen."

"Never said she was, Marvin, never said. Someone, possibly, but not me."

He kissed her other cheek. The two women in his life and neither one could be relied upon to lie as they were supposed to, to help him save face. On the other hand, it would make his life that much easier if he'd learn to lie to himself, and therefore, everyone else, that much more convincingly.

That had been Tuesday last. He should have seen it coming; they all should have. She was not, as she often insisted, often joked, two hundred fifteen; but she could have been, could have made it if she'd tried; he should have helped her try, should have willed her into trying. He'd known her for eleven years, an eternity perhaps, but he knew nothing about her. Who and what and where and when and why? Dandelions, they had talked dandelions. Rent strikes. There had been a Mr. Fitzgerald once, children once, Imogene, Sheppard, Ashlyn, Kaylee, a pet rabbit, a pair of married rats, because of course why not? a house once, a home, on some golden prairie or some immeasurable expanse, a growing list of relations, ancestors going back to a biblical past, seafaring adventurers, discoverers of things vast. Tuesday last, and he was beginning to forget what the intervening days signified, underscored, pointed out. Memory or resourcefulness, his body had little to work with to work past. She had been young once. He, Canna, his brother, Mr. Lee, everyone else on the planet.

The road had turned into freeway for the last couple of miles. Traffic starts to crowd in on him on either side. Maybe this wasn't such a good idea, after all. The traffic heading home would be worse.

> *Killed the czar and his ministers*
> *Anastasia screamed in vain ...*
>
> *I watched with glee*
> *While your kings and queens*
> *Fought for ten decades*
> *For the gods they made*

I shouted out,
Who killed the Kennedys?
When after all
It was you and me

He feels a pinch in his chest. He lets go of the steering wheel and grabs at himself as if to shake himself loose of wild notions. That his mood swings are a thing of the past, that he and his wife are in love again *("To everything — turn, turn, turn / There is a season — turn, turn, turn.")*, that unlike everyone else he can dip into life's well endlessly, that his neighbors think him gallant and bold instead of pig-headed and a failure, that he still has the time to live off the meager promises of youth *("A time to be born, a time to die / A time to plant, a time to reap")*, that he can squander and idle at leisure, that his wife's hands aren't coarse-looking and beginning to spot, that he doesn't chafe at their touch, that the turns of his life have been the right ones after all, *("A time to kill, a time to heal / A time to laugh, a time to weep")*, that the accumulating hoard of experience that is everyone's due isn't in his case down to perishable goods, that he has a right to live inside his own skin, that joy and bliss are possibilities available to everyone, that the evening and morning of his days aren't quite over *("And a time for every purpose under heaven")*, that when he delves into his wallet he doesn't always come up with small change, that he can still corner the market, some market, any market, that intimacy isn't a lie cowards cling to because they refuse to grow up *("A time of war, a time of peace / A time of love, a time of hate")*, that innocence isn't solely the purview of children or half-wits, that he no longer has to mask the fact he loathes half the planet, that he can punch out with impunity the next smart-alecky kid who talks back to him, that he has untapped filial reserves for parents in an old folks home half a country away (*"A time to build up, a time to breakdown / A time to dance, a time to mourn"*), that he doesn't have to be stinking drunk anymore to tell the truth, the whole truth and nothing but the truth, that when people say they are doing the best they can everyone understands it's a lie, that his future isn't martyred to the past (*"A time to gain, a time to lose / A time to rend, a time to sew"*), that he doesn't have to atone for sins petty or grand he can't remember ever committing, that otherwise chaste women would abandon long-term marriages willy-nilly if he'd just ask, that he, too, is allowed the mercy of letting a higher power do with him as He wilt, that Jesus-Fucking-H-Christ he can have it all to do again (*"A time to love, a time to hate / A time for peace, I swear it's not too late"*), that he can turn over at night, breathe in a lung full of fresh air and let himself be.

The sun is lower on the horizon. His left hand is back on the steering wheel, the right at his crotch, pulling at the cloth there, giving himself some air. The next turn on the road will bring him unto California Street and then Main Street on the left. He shifts a little in the front seat, sticky with sweat, and the constriction in his chest melts away as though he'd imagined it. He looks about him, a bit too urgently, as if he's lost something. The pain is gone and with it whatever fleeting thoughts the idea of impending doom pricked into being. He lowers the window and feels the smell of the ocean wash over him. The local train zips by cutting inland. He smiles at no one in particular and steps on the accelerator.

You

The day is brisk and the summer endless. Autumn is late in coming, the beaches are clean, and everywhere you look miles of sunlight. Even the pigeons are content for once to stay aloft riding mild winds in dazzling perspectives instead of landing to peck at tossed-away stuff that isn't really there. That's what the season's been so far.

A scent of something nameless is in the air. Earth and sky and nature itself, and threaded through these, fresh air, if air could be said to have a scent. Orchestras of strange familiar birds ride steady wind-swept currents. Closing my eyes, I envision a happiness I would not have thought possible.

And still he's out there, waiting to come through that one door, the one I've never left open. I can only hope that he hasn't given up yet, that it's the blind intersections that keep him turning in the wrong direction.

A few swimmers are out beyond the breakers and solitary boats brave water and winds that will soon bring in storms. The sky is a cathedral of light.

No wonder everyone dreams of ending up here. So will you. So will you.

The Architecture of Heaven

(A short science fiction novel in thirteen neatly paired chapters. An Epigraph. A Preamble. A Prologue. And two, count them, three Interludes. And an Unnecessary Aside.)

Epigraph. To every ω-consistent recursive class κ of *formulae* there correspond recursive *class signs* r, such that neither v Gen r nor Neg (v Gen r) belongs to Flg (κ) (where v is the *free variable* of r). – Kurt Gödel

Preamble. Little errors in the beginning, said the great Mangenot of M'rnýth, apostate and saint, can lead to even greater ones in the end. The ÅmБr'Rrøth Campaign was a colossal blunder from beginning to end but a beginning nonetheless.

Prologue. The sun crested the hilltops. A cold front developed, thunderstorms predicted. But not here and not now, not at this time and not in this place. The sun set and it was night again. No one dreamed of rain.

– Why now? Why you?

– My country needs me.

– We need you too.

– We've had this — why argue? what would be the point? — this ... this conversation before. The outcome's not going to change for having it again. The Lady —

– The Lady? Bah! This is the Emperor's doing.

– Quiet woman ... you never know who's —

– Why should I care? she cried, throwing open the nearest window. You, all of you. Idiots, blackguards —

– Stop it! he growled, reaching out to grab at her elbow and drag her back in. I'll be gone, however long it takes, but you'll still be here ... think of the children, think of Gran and Nana, think of —

– I am thinking of them, I'm the only one thinking of them. You —

– I'm doing what's been ordained ... pre-ordained.

– Pre-ordained! You sound —

– It's done, woman, done.

She threw herself to the floor. No one listens, she cried, no one.

Chapter One. Deep in the molten core of the planet in the region of space named after Him, in thrall to His inmost nature, deep in the fathomless surrender of the molten core, the Mad God ÅmБr'Rrøth slumbered.

Liquid.

Golden.

Wholly other.

ÅmБr'Rrøth, Lord of All, Providence's Oversoul, slept and dreamed...

At long last, the Drumlanrig would pay. At long last, His revenge would be complete. At long last, He would be at peace. At long last, He would be complete.

ÅmБr'Rrøth slept and dreamed, slept and plotted, millennia upon untold millennia.

Meanwhile the Drumlanrig conquered the skies. Seized and subjugated.

Chapter Two. Crossing into ÅmБr'Rrøth territory the Drumlanrig fleet blotted the stars like cépheid mites swarming a P'skan plain. DST and SVD battlecruisers. Starfighters (Hellion and Freynon class). Taskforce troop carriers and company haulers, defensive and offensive frigates. Armored Dix barges, landing transports, boarding craft, escort and support ships, tractor arrays. Ch'dw'ck heavy-duty bombers, launching platforms, shield generators, fortified deflectors. Destroyer formations, fighter divisions, combat wings. Fifty-three hundred seventy-six strike squadrons, one thousand twelve drovers apiece. Regimental shock troops, primary and secondary annihilator battalions. P'skan trackers and harassers. Go'dren Skullkers, Goshawk Harridans, Poniard Witches. Berserkers. Raiders. PlanetKillers. Tachyon cannons (stationary and mobile), high altitude meson torpedoes, killsat interceptors and low altitude atmospheric depth charges. Orbiting gunnery and artillery emplacements. Airborne siege engines, reinforced drones, snare bombs, viral sweep mines, neural grenades dispensers, synaptic disrupters, missile carriers, strategists, tacticians, maintenance personnel.

On the command ship *Kooning'sBrow* Admiral Bryce beamed. She had finally been given free rein to fight the war as she saw fit. She would carry the battle to the ÅmБr'Rrøth in a way they would admire. No more feints and stratagems, no more weak-willed diplomacy and spin. A real war. At last.

Chapter Three. A mad war. It would not end well.

Chapter Four. ÅmБr'Rrøth, the Mad God, slept and dreamed, slept and plotted, wrestling with an unholy urge to prostrate Himself and pray. But what, in any case, in any and every dimension of his dimensionless being, did He have to request of Himself worth giving, worth receiving? Sin, sin not, sinning.

He was beginning to think of Himself as ... a disappointment of some kind. Something was missing from His Godhead. Reaching out into Infinity there was the insubstantial edge of ... Something Other than Himself. How could this be? Primary Being equaled Primary Actuality, Prime Actuality, Prime Being. Was He not Everything That Existed and Everything That Did Not? How then could there be Something Other than that Something Other that was Himself and Himself Not? He was aware, nonetheless, that He existed someWhere in someCapacity bound by someThing somePlace. More important, He was beginning to suspect He was nothing more than some sort of supercomplex conjugate. Part of a set of one and one other, an imaginary one (and one other), conjured, summoned, pivoting round some origin, some root cause, contrary, inverse, the polar disagreement of a polar disagreement, an unsingular singularity's unpaired half. The thought terrified Him. Someone, somewhere, would stumble upon That About which Nothing Greater Could be Conceived and It would include Him as one of its constituent parts. He would be reduced, downgraded, no longer He but another he. Someone had made a terrible mistake; someone must be made to pay. 'Not for your sake did He create the world: for His sake only, for His sake alone, an ornament to Himself.' The

108

idea of ornaments to Himself, true enough, required reciprocity, a necessary relationship permitted as one permits the ghostly hugs of brain-dead children. As it should be. His children knew themselves, to the extent they knew anything, as the personification of otherness, that by which one thing compared itself to another. Hence their duality — and their escape into His arms. The circle squared, the universe put in balance. Nonetheless, something would not let Him go: something Other than Himself knew Him better than He knew Himself.

There it was.

And there.

And there again.

He would seek It out. He would destroy It. Even if it meant destroying Himself!

As He planned to destroy The Lady. And everything She stood for.

The Mad God laughed, wrapping Himself about His own Magnificence, His own Splendor and Being.

Chapter Five. Admiral Bryce frowned. She had hoped the fleet would have met more resistance as it made its way across enemy territory toward the ÅmБr'Rrøth homeworld. Cowards. Fainthearted, no doubt — had they had hearts — and pusillanimous to boot. She had known that all along.

– What of the worlds they've conquered, under their thumb, Senator Bess had cried.

– Impossible! Senator Valentia interjected.

– Madness! Senator Thirith thundered.

– Folly! Senator Kuttya underscored.

– Why now?

– Why not now?

– Posterity, of course, Senator Wosley conjectured, dictates that —

– Bugger posterity. It's the present moment we're discussing, the present moment we're after.

– Destiny, providence's lost child.

– Bugger destiny. Bugger providence. Bugger —

–The universe demands —

– Bugger the universe. Bugger demands. Bugger everyone but ourselves. Multiply that by any unit you'd like and we're all fucked if we don't act. Twice that number squared by its root cause.

Admiral Bryce had sneered. Pax Drumlanrig, the long arm of which stretched over hundreds of systems and thousands of worlds, had fathered these loose and baggy monsters. Old maids and babbling children. How could any of them call themselves Drumlanrig?

–The Åmƃr'Rrøth rule out of sheer spite, Admiral Bryce bellowed. They rely on wars of conquest kept alive in nightmare and childhood memory through the lethal administration of the Shrouded Hand. They've not had to face a hostile enemy — not one with the kind of firepower we can muster — in more cycles than anyone remembers.

The debate lasted until the second moon on the Emperial homeworld had waxed and waned twice in the fourth of its twelve cycles. Admiral Bryce had outworn them all. Because she had been right — she was always right. The Lady's Magistrate herself, in a rare appearance on the Presidium floor, proclaimed Her blessing upon the Admiral's motion. The Emperial Senate followed suit. It declared war on the Åmƃr'Rrøth. And there you have it, divine imprimatur and official sanction.

O Creator of Heaven and Earth: *Bring us to our knees.*

O Redeemer and Destroyer of Worlds: *Bring us to our knees.*

O Terrible and Appalling Presence: *Bring us to our knees.*

Remember not Great Lady our offenses, nor the offenses of our forefathers. / Reward us according to our readiness to submit to your will and demand nothing less than what you are willing to give. / Spare us, thy people, whom thou hast redeemed with thy blade: *Bring us to our knees.*

From allevil and from lastingever lief: Great Lady, bring us to our knees.

Saoshyant, Saoshyant.

Preparations for war had gone fairly straightforward after that, even for the Drumlanrig. The Emperium was put on full alert and taxes levied; planets, habitats and orbitals, major and minor asteroid belts were placed on military footing; strategy was codified and objectives crystallized; combatants were drafted, spies recruited, mercenaries bought out; shipyards in system after system worked incessantly to fill the increasing demand for warships commissioned by the Emperial War College; bridgeheads along the systems-wide border with the enemy were constructed and ancillary support channels secured; strategists devised textured, brutal schemes to defeat the ÅmБr'Rrøth piecemeal, system by system or all at once — a full-scale frontal assault on their homeworld; after which any outworld principality or dependency with plans for counterattack or revenge, manifest or implied, would be wiped out mercilessly and a beaten zone laid out. At home, personal communications were monitored, anti-war sentiments ferreted out and unlikely treason quashed; attitudes were molded, allegiances established, public opinion contrived; martial drums beat at every occasion, official and otherwise, and the young were schooled in the mythic battles of the Empire's founding; heart- and hinterland were squeezed for every available resource that could possibly serve the war; the myriad races of the Emperium, all too eager, it seemed, to bear the burdens of empire thrust upon them, complied wholeheartedly. Admiral Bryce got her war.

But on the bridge of *Kooning'sBrow* Admiral Bryce was far from satisfied. Why had they not come across any sign of the enemy? Scout ships? Feints and probes at weakness in the fleet? The ÅmБr'Rrøth, Admiral Bryce had warned the fleet's strategists and tacticians, were not a species they could afford to underestimate. Where were they?

Chapter Six. ÅmБr'Rrøth, the Shape of Infinity, the One True God, slept and dreamed, slept and plotted, the Fullness of Being like gossamer wings across His mind's Eye. Every God needed a vehicle, an instrument, a go-between or agent: something or someone to uphold His existence. Without a people to love and worship Him, to venerate and fear Him, the burden of His Magnificence could not cross from one soul to another, from one part of creation to any other, from any part of eternity to any other and beyond. Without exemplary faith or stated belief, a God was left with nothing but the mute existential declaration of things. Kill the believer and you killed the God. The idea of God was the content of an act of understanding that left no further question to be resolved. What would happen my children if the universe gave birth to the insinuation of a pullulating godhead? The universe needed a First Agent and a Last End. There could be only one God in the Heavens. He would not be superseded, He would not be surpassed. The Drumlanrig had usurped His place in the heavens by invoking Hers in His stead. For this they must be made to pay. For this She must die. After today

112

The Lady would be no more than a token, a portent, a reproof without teeth.

Interlude One

– Who made the world and the Great City?

– ÅmБr'Rrøth .

– Who is ÅmБr'Rrøth?

– The Creator of all the ÅmБr'Rrøth.

– Who are the ÅmБr'Rrøth?

– A desperately simple people, mighty unto themselves, craving salvation.

– Why did ÅmБr'Rrøth create the ÅmБr'Rrøth?

– To serve Him in this world and worship at His knee in the next.

– What must we do to attain both ends?

– Submit to His will without question.

– How shall we know how to submit?

– From the Shrouded Hand, through whom ÅmБr'Rrøth speaks.

– What is ÅmБr'Rrøth?

– Love everlasting.

– Does ÅmБr'Rrøth know all?

– Our most secret thoughts, every deed, every word, every here and every thereafter.

Chapter Seven. Vogel had been following Duncan around the galaxy for so long he might as well have been chasing his own tail. He'd forgotten what had started it all, the why of it. Still, he persevered. At some point Duncan would hit pay dirt, at some point the Holy Grail — or the equivalent thereof out there in the

Outer Reaches. In any case, there was so little of his life left to restore, or crawl back into, he might as well fly by the seat of his pants, no matter how many times they'd need mending.

He stole a glance at the starfinder whose readout Duncan studied intently as so many glyphs on a M'rnýth wall — a spiraling wall of stars to port, a giant sun glowing blue in the distance, everywhere else empty space. Just as quickly he shifted back to the space in front of him. He was supposed to be navigating through mindsense alone. But the urgency of their mission unnerved him, and he kept trying to gain reassurance from his physical surroundings, the chair beneath him, the flight cabin, the congealing flotsam of a flat expanding universe.

– We're almost there, Duncan said, more wishful thinking than absolute fact. Vogel did not respond, gazing fixedly at the inch of space in front of him. Mindsense split in two Vogel navigated deep space, carefully maneuvering through stellar winds, as he probed the Straits of Galatea for any sign of the flotilla of starships that only now made its way determinedly towards its deadly purpose, the extermination of the ÅmБr'Rrøth — it had to be intercepted, it had to be warned.

Duncan spit out a P'skan curse. Fighters, DreadWidows all, were dropping out of nowhere athwart their sunscoop, foreguns firing. He cursed again. No time to figure out how they had been discovered. The shriek of metal signaled that one of the polymer sails had been hit by incoming fire, and on the periphery of vision, the flash of dré'chcanons. Vogel's hands swept across the navigation panel, manual overrides flowing into action. The susurration of shields coming on, shields that had been dropped for maximum thrust and drive, was felt like a whispered sigh across the back of his neck. If life could only be so promising.

They could stand and fight, and, outgunned and outclassed,

go out as heroes — but heroes needed survivors to sing of noble acts and valiant deeds, and in battle the Åmƃr'Rrøth believed in swift death — or they could risk an interstitial jump at close range to the DreadWidows. There would be no way of telling if the pull of the interstitial engines would drag any of the fighters along in their wake until it was too late, the deadly fight carried on in the differential planes of interstitial space, where dimensions arched and curved so that you could end up shooting your ass out from underneath yourself.

Duncan fired up the jump engines as Vogel valiantly tested one flanking maneuver after another. The sunscoop thrummed as the g-forces of interstitial space began their inward pull. DreadWidows angled and banked slantwise in five different directions, scurrying as far and as fast as they could as the jump gate reached critical (.00001±3.55523978 at phase transition). The DreadWidows' mission had been to harass and stall, which, if everything went as Åmƃr'Rrøth decreed meant bedlam and blood sport, not hot pursuit through the twenty-six dimensions of interstitial space.

Vogel experienced a moment of wrenching vertigo as the pull of the jump turned into a precipitous drop into interstitial space. The war had not yet begun, the ringing declarations of war had barely been uttered, banners flying, trumpets blowing, jingoistic fellow feelings translating into a higher percentage of votes for the war-favoring parties, the display of force just that, shadow play and dumb show, a self-propitiating ritual of chauvinistic pride in full gear, and here he was tumbling head over high end into the role of personal savior to his own race. The Lords of Drumlanrig had badly underestimated the Åmƃr'Rrøth. The Byzantine rites of war of the Drumlanrig, sacramental and traditional, which they shared reaching back no doubt to a common ancestor along this arm of the Permian Cluster, were a mystery to the ÅmБr'Rrøth. War was war when the ÅmБr'Rrøth waged it. But the Drumlanrig, whose arrogance could be said to reach into all twenty-six dimensions of interstitial space and the eleven of normal spacetime, could always be counted on to define reality in terms of their own collective delusions. Not so with the ÅmБr'Rrøth. The war was just beginning but as the sunscoop traversed interstitial space toward the disputed border between System Drumlanrig and the Suzerainty of ÅmБr'Rrøth, Vogel hoped it was not too late. Not too late, indeed.

Interlude Two

–What are we by nature?

–We are made in the image of ÅmБr'Rrøth.

–What does it mean to be created in His image?

–That we are free to be deadly in submission to His will.

–Why then do we live out of harmony with His will?

–We have misused our freedom and made wrong choices.

–Why do we misuse our freedom?

–We are afraid of our nature.

–Why do we make wrong choices?

–We are broken and know not what to choose.

–What help is there for us?

– Submission, deference, assent.

– How did ÅmБr'Rrøth first reach out his hand to us?

– By revealing Himself to the children of the Great City.

–What did we learn from His revelation to the ÅmБr'Rrøth?

–That He is The One, seen and unseen.

–What does this mean?

–That the universe is a cruel master.

– What does this mean regarding the ÅmБr'Rrøth's place in the universe?

–That it belongs to us, bestowed by His hand.

–What does this mean about life?

–That it must submit to an all-consuming will, and to make of that reverence but a stepping stone into eternity.

–What is our duty to our neighbors?

–To ensure their submission to ÅmБr'Rrøth as indefatigably as we do; to carry the peace of the sword to all corners of His creation; and to guarantee they obey those who wield Eternity's Sword on His behalf.

– And what is our duty to ourselves?

–To increase our birthright and enlarge our legacy.

– Since we do not constantly obey His decrees, are they useful at all?

– Yes: so that we may be brought to our knees in need of eternal damnation.

An Unnecessary Aside. Vogel once heard a Euleurian priestess attribute the witlessness of fools to what 'they didn't know they didn't know they didn't know.' He was perplexed. What didn't he know he didn't know he didn't know? What silliness. What rank drivel. He ran after the priestess and demanded an explanation. Her guards dragged him away. What priestly gibberish, what ecclesiastical double talk. He went back to a life lived largely out of reflex — but a haunted man. He contrived the idea of turning around and seeing the back of his head, of being alive during his own funeral, of getting a glimpse of life with the veil drawn back. Clearly, he was not to be trusted around the clerical set.

Of Duncan we know very little. Perhaps that's to the wise. He was tall. That much we understand. Neatly built, quarter-moon eyes. Twenty-one wives. The universe being large and wide enough, he never had to see any one of them after the first dewy hours of his honeymoons. Premarital sex had been outlawed since the Cinquecento Wars of Attrition. Perhaps that had something to do with it. Fact is, he never envied the simple life.

Chapter Eight. Thankfully, Vogel was an accomplished navigator. The sensory overload of interstitial space, of navigating twenty-six dimensions — distance and proximity curvilinear and circumflex; distortion of spacetime at zero mass and three units of spin; Planck length and magnitude equal to the square of nodal scale (Bolyai's constant), including any and all asymmetrical polyhedral domain minima; each nodal thread felt throughout the synapses as so many pinpricks across neural strands — expected to tax most men to near exhaustion, interstitial jumps of necessity being of short duration, mindsense or not, made Vogel only slightly more temperamental than usual.

– Dr'lan be praised!

Blasphemy! thought Vogel. Duncan had used The Lady's recondite name. But he must have sensed it before it came into view. A DreadNought, insinuating itself, slowly, deliberately, into the space before them. Not possible. Battleships were not supposed to move so precisely, with so much calculation; they were not designed to survive the countervailing forces of interstitial space. Speed, maneuverability, and no small pretense that the impossible was possible: smaller ships could do it (sunscoops, starriders, any one of the sixteen classes of HellCats). But not this, nothing this immense, spreading across the horizon like a stain. And heading toward them. They were, after all, slipping through nowhere, the space between space, a seam in the universe that existed because sentient beings fixated on roaming the stars had needed it and found it where it was not supposed to be.

The DreadNought crawled to a stop in front of them. Vogel's mindsense tingled incessantly as the sunscoop's sensors informed him they were being scanned. The sunscoop came to a sudden halt as if grasped in an invisible viselike grip. Not possible. Not in interstitial space. His mind raced. The information they had been given — newly developed ÅmБr'Rrøth technology, lethal weaponry, indomitable battleships — had been right all along.

< Would you die for The Lady, Efrem Vogel? >

Vogel shivered involuntarily. He had not so much heard the words as felt them, white hot, across the nerve bundles at the upper part of his spinal cord. He gagged.

Duncan was yelling in his ear. Do something! desperately trying to deploy weaponry, something, anything that would work. It didn't matter. Their ship was effectively dead.

< Would you die for The Lady, Efrem Vogel? >

Duncan clutched at the back of his neck. He'd heard it, too. Do something, damn it, do something! Duncan cried. Which Vogel did. Across from him a small series of neural circuitry switched off in his friend's brain. Duncan slumped to the floor. He'd be out for an hour or so. By then they'd be back home and laughing at the whole thing over beer and streusel. I have to do this alone, I have to do this alone, Vogel thought, as though apologizing to his friend. Seems he was always apologizing, had been apologizing ever since he'd met Duncan eighteen cycles ago. That was, he supposed, the nature of their relationship. In exchange for... Well, he'd traveled the known universe, even if that meant only that part of the universe otherwise known as Aleph Prime, his own spiraling galaxy. Vast enough, and with an abundance

119

of worlds to engage a man's imagination for a lifetime. And if he was to keep that promise to himself, and to Duncan, they were both going to have to survive. But how?

He sensed shields being dropped on the other ship.

< Welcome little one, welcome. >

He had to act fast. He concentrated. I still have a few tricks up my sleeve, he thought. He would have to be careful, he told himself, as the molecules of his body began to translate across shifting dimensions.

Vogel found a place not otherwise occupied by solid matter within which to materialize. A command station of some sort. Murrian 'droids, semi-sentient biomachinery normally used for low-end outworld maintenance in systems under ÅmБr'Rrøth control, scurried about oblivious to his sudden appearance. He sensed no one else on board.

Vogel grimaced, pulling absently at an ear. He felt caged and ill at ease, aware of elbows and knees, afraid to take a step, afraid of his own sense of gravity. This was more disheartening than he cared to admit. ÅmБr'Rrøth High Command had obviously turned over the running of a DreadNought, one of such daunting capabilities, to a small contingent of servo 'bots. In the coming battle with the Drumlanrig, there would be spilled blood, scorched and ruined flesh on one side, and on the other, scrap metal and robot parts. Things could not possibly get worse. He would have thought the whole thing impossible under the worst of circumstances, but he had experienced too much this day to think anything was beyond belief or ÅmБr'Rrøth guile.

Now what? Mindsense had no effect on artificial life forms, bio-engineered or not. And he doubted they were programmed to answer questions from a stranger, especially one they didn't

120

have the decency to acknowledge. No doubt their mission had been accomplished, the sunscoop in tow, Duncan tucked away in a holding cell somewhere. What possible threat could he be? He felt a minor shift in the ship's orientation and spin — the DreadNought was moving.

Interlude Three

– What is sin?

– The seeking of our own perfection by our own will instead of ÅmБr'Rrøth's.

– How does sin have power over us?

– By causing us to lose our liberty every time we fail to submit to His will.

– What is redemption?

– The act of ÅmБr'Rrøth which sets us free from the power of evil and our inability to submit to His will.

– How does ÅmБr'Rrøth prepare us for redemption?

– He sent us the Shrouded Hand to call us back to His lap.

– What is the Shrouded Hand?

– The soil upon which His will was first sown.

– And how are we to recognize them?

– By the Hand that Wields the Whip, to which all the ÅmБr'Rrøth must submit.

– What is the mission of the Shrouded Hand?

– To restore the universe to its rightful order.

– What is the imperative of the Shrouded Hand?

– That by their guidance we may live in harmony with His will and all of His creation.

Chapter Nine. Duncan, find Duncan, he told himself.

< He is with The Lady now. >

Searing heat ... the microstructure of his brain on fire ... afferent nerve ends aflame.

– No! He glanced over at the 'droids. They paid him little attention, busy monitoring screens, 'droid beings doing 'droid things. Please not Duncan.

< He would not cry for you with such fervor. >

– How would you know?

< I know everything. >

– Well you've missed a thing or two. Duncan's my friend. More than that, he thought, even though Duncan would have balked at the notion.

< Was. >

– I don't believe you. I don't believe anything that's happening.

< You would question a God, Efrem Vogel? >

– Who are you?

< A jealous God, Efrem Vogel. A very jealous God. >

It was not a matter of evidence or proof. But this ... this thing at the center of an all-encompassing pain had killed his best friend, the one constant in his life — he would not believe a God could be so cruel.

< I am the Ground of Being, Efrem Vogel. The Shape of Infinity. Your One True God.>

– I answer only to The Lady, he challenged. It couldn't be. It could not be He.

< And soon She will answer to me. >

– Never!

< Oh, yes. Soon. >

The burning, having cycled through every neuron and synapse, every afferent and efferent pathway in his body, was making it impossible for him to think or do much but retch repeatedly

122

as he collapsed to the floor.

– Never!

< Tell me Efrem Vogel, are you not afraid of your God? > The 'voice' sounded… — sincere, and very much amused.

– You are not my God, he resisted. I told you: I answer only to The Lady.

< Which is why She must die. >

– You can't kill The Lady. Could he?

< I'm just getting started. >

He doubled up on the floor. The pain was all there was now, and the searing consciousness. Which would not let him go.

– But why, why are you doing this?

< Reality must be channeled in one direction Efrem Vogel, existence confronted with one true source. >

Why was He going on? Why was He torturing him so?

< The idea of God is the content of an act of understanding that leaves no further questions to be resolved. >

The pain continued. He should have been a husk by now, a hollowed out thing, an excuse for a human being. But the pain went on without surcease, as though there was yet more of him left to squeeze.

< The universe needs a First Agent and a Last End. There can be only one God in the Heavens, Efrem Vogel, one central point in creation toward which every will must bend.>

He was on fire, every facet of his existence, whatever was left of a self, of pure subjective being, was being seared away, purified and distilled. But into what?

< I will not be superseded. The Lady's children usurped my place in the heavens by invoking Hers in my stead. For this they — She — must be made to pay. >

None of it made sense. His best friend was dead somewhere

in the confines of this behemoth, what was left of his mind and body was being burningly sheared away, flesh by flesh, bone by bone, consciousness by excruciating consciousness — and he was being forced to listen to a lesson on theology by a Mad God.

< For this She must die. >

Efrem Vogel screamed. Or thought he did. He no longer had a mouth with which to scream, or a set of ears to register the sound. A synaptic echo? Did he have any synapses left?

< There can be only one Primary Intelligibility Efrem Vogel, one Supreme Value, one Overriding Truth. There is no need in the universe for more than One True God. The Lady must die. >

But why? Why?

< I was here first. >

No more. Dear God, any god, no more. He wanted to grieve, to mourn, to drown out the horror of what he was hearing with his own twice-desired scream.

It didn't matter. Nothing did. Efrem Vogel no longer cared who lived or died — if only he could.

< It is not your time, Efrem Vogel. I have prepared a special place for you in my plans. You will bear witness to the wholesale devastation visited upon your species, your race. You will be the instrument of my rebirth and the destruction of your kind. >

Suddenly, the pain stopped. Suddenly, Efrem Vogel was no more. Suddenly, he was everything and everywhere.

Numen.

Absolute.

Wholly other.

The Drumlanrig had planned to destroy a fleet, instead they would face an unfathomable all-pervading presence that brooked no challengers.

The one remaining speck of consciousness that had been

124

Vogel wished he had time to ponder —

The appalling majesty of being raised beyond the level of mere creature ...

The dreadful grandeur of bringing existence back into harmony with itself ...

The unspeakable splendor of being the object of Divine Will ...

To feel what a God feels — if only for a while.

But he had work to do — the excruciating unfolding of His plans — the work of ÅmБr'Rrøth, the Mad God.

He laughed at the joy of it all, a slow, low rumble.

Chapter Ten. Territorial reconnaissance, strategic insertion points, lines of engagement ... attacks of opportunity or mere chance, fixed positioning, explosive reach, damage threshold ... strategic success in any field of action is provided by consistently integrating battlefield scenarios to ends and means. ... The point of frontline survivability is made possible the extent to which lethal force can take advantage of any level of threat manifest in battlefield engagement. Decisive action is achieved, achievable, through the measured conduct of deliberate —

– Admiral Bryce?

–Yes?

–You said not to disturb you unless —

–Yes?

–Well I mean ... our scout ships Admiral ... they seemed to have detected something.

– Don't just stand there Lieutenant, out with it.

– Well I mean ... we're not sure what it is. We've never encountered anything like it, Admiral. It makes no sense. Our analyses, our territorial mappings —

– Give me that.

–Yes Admiral Bryce. … As you can see Admiral … the region circumscribing the cosmographic boundary of ÅmБr'Rrøth … seems … gives the impression … ah, that is, well it appears to be coalescing into some sort of massively ramifying Oort cloud.

–That's impossible!

–Yes Admiral Bryce. But we've double-checked the data —

– Double-check it again. … And Lieutenant — do not disturb me again unless you're absolutely sure. Is that understood, Lieutenant?

–Yes Admiral Bryce. Of course, Admiral Bryce.

Where did they find them these days? Massively ramifying my ass … where was she? … Ah, yes, battlefield survivability.

Chapter Eleven. The ÅmБr'Rrøth, pod, clade, branch and root, woke from their sleep to the sound of lunar thunder echoing on the horizon, a slow, low rumble. ÅmБr'Rrøth's laughter. The Mad God must be pleased, the war had been a good choice after all.

Chapter Twelve. At the other end of the galaxy, on the bridge of her command ship, *Kooning'sBrow*, Admiral Bryce heard it too. Inertial thrusters coming on, from the sound of it, periodically firing up to keep the ship's orientation and pitch, as it flung it-self across the stars, balanced and true. But it reminded her of something else, something she'd heard of before. Not on her homeworld, but somewhere. There was a name for that sound. Admiral Bryce shook her head. She had no time for such non-sense. She had a war to fight, to win. Some other day, perhaps, but not today.

Chapter Thirteen. A mad war. It did not end well.

126

Listen Officer

They found him on an access road that fed off the main highway. But it was too late. Listen officer, listen. He saw the police cruiser pull up next to the bus as he exited the men's room, and thought it wise to head for parts unknown. Let me ask you something officer, he'd thought of saying to the nearest one, the redheaded one, the one stroking his chin, listen officer, he'd thought of saying, shouldn't people be allowed to travel from one coast to the next if they have a mind to? How would you like it if all you were allowed to cross was from one corner of the street to the other and back again? Listen officer, how would you like it if people got the notion that was as far as you ever wanted to go, needed to go? Instead, he decided to take matters into his own hands? Who was going to miss him anyway? He hadn't been allowed a driver's license for a while. But by then he'd had his fill of driving everyone around wherever they wanted. Football games, wrestling matches, spelling bees, PTA meetings, parent-teacher nights, band practice and school plays, dance recitals, Boy Scout jamborees, hunting trips, fishing weekends, dental appointments, braces, crooked incisors and capped teeth, scrapes and strains, sprained ankles, injured knees, flu-shots, seasonal vaccinations, unexpected rashes, conjunctivitis, lockjaw, a suspected miscarriage or two, family get-togethers, dinner parties, city tours, picnics and parades, grocery shopping, bake sales, inventory clearances, graduation ceremonies, weddings, birthdays, second and third cousins, once or twice removed, formals, anniversaries, holiday gatherings, Sunday luncheons, social calls, house warmings, coffee klatches, masquerades, trysts, workaday mornings, late-evening returns. He had taken to long walks instead, wanting his feet as firmly planted on the ground as physically possible without growing roots.

He walked downwind, into a future he hoped was around a turn in the road. He spotted shin oaks ahead, leaves and branches as welcoming as hellos from strangers in the street. Here and there, a thicket of devil's walking stick. But he was probably wrong. He didn't think he was anywhere near the Piney Woods, his childhood. But perhaps he was wrong about that, too. If so, he would soon chance upon clusters of cottontails, a woodpecker or two, swooping from tree to tree. The sun would soon be lowering below the tree line and the late afternoon heat would begin to soften. As it was, the light on the horizon was much too bright. Tuck your chin in, he told himself, tuck your chin in. But the sky, the sky among a scattering of clouds was a festival of blue.

He planned to walk as far as his feet would take him, at which point he would stop and hope someone would come by with a drink of water and a bite to eat. He intended to keep moving for as long as possible, the edge of the world, where in the distance answers to all the questions he'd forgotten to ask could be glimpsed at last, questions let slip through the cracks because he'd been schooled in missed chances, answers that

128

had once or twice drifted his way like birthday balloons loose from a child's less-than-firm grip to land at his feet, teasingly like a shy-away kiss. A tender kick from weathered shoes would boot them to glide upwind and into the breeze. That they were there, within reach, was enough. He'd arrived. With more time on his hands than he could ever handle. And look, look at the view.

Journaling

April 3. I've sprung forward, like the rest of the country. Sister called again, mother's complaining that we don't visit, call enough. Lucky my dad died when he did. I left the TV on again all night. I could hear it through the thin walls that separate the living room from the bedroom. TV voices faint yet strangely distinct, what passes for crickets in the city. It's a wonder the homicide rate has remained relatively flat for the last few years.

April 4. I've never seen a blind man stumble. I do, however, hate the way they stare blankly ahead or past you while you wait for them to finish what they're saying. Couldn't do it. I stand out enough as it is.

April 5. Bury me when I'm dead: to such resolve comes all purpose.

April 6. It's always important to note the time and place when bad news arrives — if for no other reason than to also note that time and place are of little importance. Bad news arrives anytime of the week but rarely on weekends, not at the stroke of this or that hour, not when we're about to turn the page, put the book down and call it a day. Context is everything.

April 7. Terrible accident outside, the sound of the thing like a punch against unforgiving flesh. Everyone except the two people involved is taking out his or her cell phone, calling someone, imagining they care. Someone, young from the sound of it, is crying hysterically. I cry, if I cry at all, in private. It's unnerving to think that anything so inconsequential as another car accident in another L.A. street, something so dull and routine (think masturbating, think love and intimacy while pretending you're not masturbating), can strike someone so deep.

April 8. A band of new and old gold is discernible through morning cloud. A car whizzes by trying to beat the morning rush. The couple in the house next to me isn't up yet. The redhead across the way has yet to lock her door on her way to work. Water boils on the stove. The day beckons.

April 9. Breakfast of eggs and bacon, despite doctor's warning. Extra cup of coffee. I have this growing suspicion that someone else is looking out through my eyes, as though I'm spying in on myself, as though I've done something corrupt. Who am I kidding? When have I ever done anything of consequence, morally reprobate or just plain wrong? I'd have to shave myself toe to crotch, knuckle to armpit, to smell like everyone else, to be like everyone else, enterprising and unscrupulous.

April 10. Should have borrowed the book instead of paying full price.

April 12. Bill called. Usual BS. Said she read that if one's stool floats instead of sinking to the bottom of the toilet bowl, this had less to do with one's overall fiber intake than a sign of one's general intelligence. A $500,000 federal grant, no kidding. Correlations have yet to be teased out, she said, enough to get some lucky bastard another grant for further studies. Can't believe I'm mulling over anything Bill has ever said. I'm as boring as everyone, everything I claim to hate.

April 13 - 14. Joshua Tree National Park. Rock climbing; friend's idea. "Ocotillo plants and jumping cholla cactus, California juniper, pinyon pine, washes, playas, alluvial fans, desert varnish, igneous and metamorphic rocks." If I wanted the running commentary I'd be home watching the Nature Channel. You'd think he was being paid by the U.S. Park Service. The point of being out in nature is that you get to experience it at any number of individual levels and depths, your level, your depth. Can't sleep. Would love to take a walk, but what if I get lost. I could make my friend go with me but then that would mean two people lost. The desert at night: the Milky Way does exist.

April 15. The rain hasn't stopped coming down for weeks now. Someone lied to us. They promised the world's cleansing would come with fire next time. Long email from M. telling me, yet again, why we broke up, why she had to move to Utah to make sure she wouldn't be tempted back. A low threshold for ambivalence, that's what drove you away, not some scramble for distance or the long view. She'd accuse me of being up to my old tricks again. She'd be right. Your genitals say feed me, you brain starve me. Maybe it's the other way around or maybe it makes no difference at all.

April 17. I drove by it recently. Not by accident; everyone says that. I meant to do it, wanting to see if memory is half the bitch she pretends to be. I remembered it as a light mustard color; now it's the color of a rusted nail. The front porch, once open and airy, is encased in railing and grillwork.

Note to self: Does he think he's helping us remember that we're mortal, that we die once and once only, not repeatedly like on television?

Note to self: Don't forget to add butter, scratch that, margarine to the grocery list.

April 18. The year is older. Summer is no more than a memory and children everywhere are disappointed because they never got the hang of it, its perfect form, and soon some grown up, someone they will never like, never hope to like, will say "Now boys and girls, turn to page eight." I am on my back in the middle of the living room. I've moved all the furniture to the far side of every wall. The light from the kitchen rounds the half wall and spills like white shadow, a ghost of a ghost. I'm not alone, not totally in the dark. I'm not crazy, although I may well be insane. A bus passes by. The floorboards beneath me shake like a body exposed to the cold. The silence echoes and stirs. Space is becoming time and time space. Time and space, intimacy and immensity, one and the same. I've never pretended to like people and yet here I am eager for some company, itching to reach over in the dead of night, across clean floor and empty reaches to touch flesh that touches back. Wonder what's next.

Note to self: This isn't going to end well, we're all going to end up as disappointed as a marriage that promises love everlasting and delivers a few broken ribs instead.

Note to self: Stop writing your notes to self on post-it notes; they leave a trail, and people are likely to misunderstand.

April 20. Threw your ass out, did she? my father said on hearing the news that his middle child was as unlucky in love as every other bastard on the planet, and you always willing to piss in a cup if she even hinted she was thirsty. True, I countered, but for a moment there, she came to believe I *had* offered her my last drink of water. That was what? three years ago? We laughed as though we'd shared a truth about the world in general.

April 21. Walked to the westernmost end of the City today, hoping that if I stared long enough at the horizon I'd see the world tilt toward some endpoint. The sun, a quarter of its usual size, hovered over the sky like something suggestive of light. I've walked the City end-to-end lengthwise and always the same coastline. I could write a history of that journey I suppose. When it started and where it will end is a mystery, and like other mysteries, endless and survivable. Sometimes as I walk the City something monstrous and swollen takes hold of me. I would call it longing or some other hunger but the romance of such things is beyond me. I looked out to the horizon: it had not yet tilted.

April 23. The Metrolink in summer. I sit next to an elderly woman in a rain slicker. She feigns a smile and shrinks into her seat. In the seat in front of me an African-American woman with a bandanna swaddled around her head is Witnessing to a patient man in a business suit about His coming. The man frowns and looks out the window. She Witnesses with more fervor. An anorexic youth's hair is cut like a three-tiered cake, a streak of lightning dangling from his ear. His friend, thinner still, sports a flat top, skintight golf pants and tri-colored shoes. Three Mexican men in white shirts, black pants and bowties sit stiffly so as not to wrinkle their uniforms. A woman has strapped herself into a pair of minuscule shorts. She's wearing a puny bra; you can see everything through the gauzy blouse. The sheer fabric cuts in half nipples the color of sunburn; they look like twin Kilroys peeking up over their little fences of lace. A white-haired man scolds the woman next to him. Two women clatter in low gutturals over the heads of children on their laps while they visit mayhem on every passenger within eyeshot with toy pistols in toy hands. A man looks as though he's slept in his shoes, hair curling like smoke. A young woman with hair the color of ice-tea, the athletic neck supple above the collar line, glances about at each stop as though she's forgotten where she's headed. A business man reads his newspaper. Another man stands looking at nothing. Someone giggles. I look out the window to see if I am anywhere nearer my destination. The woman next to me startles as though I were a huge animal thing throwing a paw out in her direction.

April 24. A noxious layer of smog papers the sky; storm clouds building can be glimpsed through the haze like faded crayon. A hint of rain flavors the air yet the ground dances heat off its back so that at a distance everything sways and waves, waves and sways, like drag queens on parade. Earthquake weather. I feel feverish. The unseasonal heat. I am constantly surprised by the lack of surprise in the City's weather patterns.

April 25. Imagine tall sails on taller masts tacking against high winds testing their crews' mettle. Imagine me wading out past the reef line and breaking toward their keels, testing mine.

April 27. My neighbors are quiet for once. The Iranian couple next door, longwinded and shrill in English and Farsi, are inside with the windows closed. In the corner, there's a polyglot apartment building that's trying to keep up appearances. Most of the tenants are spectral figures. You spot them furtively emptying out their trash and retrieving mail at odd hours of the evening. They walk crabwise, heads down, hugging the sides of the building as though to blend in. They return hellos, when they do, to your chin. They live, I presume, on mouse savings or the generosity of the state. No one remembers them ever having moved in. They came with the building, like the kitchen sink.

April 28. Yesterday the twenty-something kid from across the way stopped me in the driveway to inform me he'd landed a job with an annual salary of $256,000. It's about time, he crowed. And here I am, between jobs, as they say out here, and not a dog to sing to. The kid glowed. I'm glad for you, I said, lying to one of us. I noticed that the hair at the back of his head was thinning. Should I have said something?

April 29. Possibly I don't trust my instincts, possibly I don't trust my sense of proportional response, possibly I'm afraid of the dark.

April 30. We'd like to be able to trust, we'd like to believe in something, even if it's believing in not believing, in belief as an afterthought. We're a nation of ironists.

Beep, beep, beep. Beep, beep, beep. Beep, beep, beep. Beep, beep, beep, beep, beep, beep, beep, beep, beep, beep, beep. For what seemed like an eternity. Aren't there laws against that? Beep, beep, beep.

The Noontime Brightness Will Rise forThee

He arrived bereft of nothing lonely in parts turned the corner two lights up from where he expected to be and parked. *Main Street Lodge.* Farther down the same half-block: *Main Street Café.* Two storefronts down: *Main Street Uniform & Shoes.* He was nowhere near a main street or the celebrated Main Street. A joke part of the city then, and he on a lark. He let the engine idle and fiddled with the radio, as though there was a song he wanted to hear, as though interrogating one station after another would work its magic or find its mark. He turned the engine off and reached for his laptop on the passenger seat.

"Nights? One or two?"

"Six. Prime numbers I believe have been temporarily outlawed."

The man behind the counter frowned, not a categorical no, but a definite sign he wasn't in the business of being entertained, not this time of day and possibly not any other, yes, yes, it was his job to be gracious, but certain conditions applied, and asked him the usual set of questions: name, license number, credit card information, billing address, minimum length of stay, right, right, he'd volunteered that, smoking or non-smoking, facing the mountains or pool and courtyard?

"Mountains." The sun would rise poolside he calculated quickly. He wasn't enamored of morning sun on his face even if from behind a double wall of hotel curtains.

"Sign here and initial here and here. Local calls are free, long-distance carries a small charge. We offer complimentary continental breakfast, 6:30 to 10:30 a.m., complimentary Wi-Fi. You're here. Drive to the end of the driveway, turn right and right again, there should be open parking in front of your room, second floor to the left. Any questions, don't hesitate to call. Keys, keys. Enjoy your stay."

The room was well apportioned, smart, clean — a floating flat-screen TV unobtrusive against a far wall, hard-wearing nightstands glistening, brass lamps, patterned shades, a more than serviceable breakfront, an oval table next to the window for his laptop or a nightcap, the odd mezzotint on the odd wall, bed and pillows cloud-bound, carpeting that softened every footstep — not what you'd expect out here past the outer bounds of the easternmost rim of nowhere. The bathroom smelled of soap. He put his laptop on the table and his travel bag at the foot of the bed next to the wall. Conceivably the next six days wouldn't be too bad. Who said chance decisions were a thing of the past? He sat on the edge of the bed and took off shoes and socks. Coughing goats and unruly nursemaids, he thought, and rummaged through the carry-on to come up with a bottle of scotch. He supposed he would have to walk

140

barefoot to find where the ice machine was. He was not, when it came to these things, a fanatic, but neither did he like his liquor lukewarm. What the hell, this one time wouldn't hurt; he didn't feel like going out, even if for a short jaunt. He drew the curtains open. The mountains looked like mountains, only farther off, palms trees, of course, and stands of flowering climbers and shrubs someone other than he would be able to name. The horizon was the horizon was the horizon, the deceptive vistas, the unfailing quality of light. The sound of street traffic, far off and muffled, anticipated other sounds. He wished ... well, there were lots of things he wished. He sipped at his drink, taking the time to savor the wood, the smoke, the individual notes. He could get some things right after all. He drew the curtains shut.

∞

EXTERNAL EXAMINATION. PRELIMINARY ASSESSMENT. EXCERPT. Time of autopsy: 10:45 a.m. Personal effects include one black brushed domed tungsten wedding ring, standard size 10, worn on the ring finger of the right hand and one 1-inch wide expandable wristband left wrist. Seven 1.5-inch wide brown leather straps are cinched around 1) the neck, 2) upper chest, at the sternum, 3) mid-abdomen, an inch below the ribcage, and 4) fastened to each of the four extremities. Dark-red ligature marks, identified throughout the report as Ligature A, B, C, D, E, F, and G, horizontal in orientation, disclosed themselves upon removal of the brown leather straps. Lividity is fixed at the distal portions of the limbs. Skin of the neck below marks and surrounding tissue reveal petechial hemorrhaging. No other signs of struggle prominent. The buckles on the leather straps exhibit traces of blood, possibly the victim's. Body that of a normally developed white male 72 inches, 190 pounds. Appearance consistent with recorded age of 36 years. Irises blue, corneas muddy somewhat. Hair dark-blonde, approximately two inches in length. Genitalia that of an adult male, no evidence of injury or harm. Pubic hair appears to have been cropped, before or after time of death still to be determined. Limbs, symmetrically developed, show no evidence of previous impairment. Fingernails average length, beds bluish in nature. No residual scars, markings or tattoos.

INTERNAL EXAMINATION. SUMMARY. *Head/Central Nervous System*: The brain weighs 1,360 grams and is within normal limits. Every other structure normal and anatomically configured. Spinal cord not dissected. *Respiratory System/ Throat Structures*: Oral cavity displays no lesions or obstruction of the airways. No injuries are observed and there are no mucosal lesions. Hyoid bone, thyroid and cricoid cartilages exhibit visible fractures, cause yet to be determined. Lungs exhibit signs of minor lung disorder consistent with some sort of smoking habit or average-to-protracted exposure to air pollution, otherwise unremarkable. Transverse fractures of right ribs five (5) and six (6). Preliminary analysis suggests perimortem cause. Direct impact possible source. Further analysis warranted. *Cardiovascular System*: Heart weighs 262 grams and is of normal size and configuration. No evidence of atherosclerosis, cardiomegaly, cardio-myopathy (dilated, hypertrophic or restricted), pericarditis, pericardial effusion or Marfan syndrome present. *Gastrointestinal System*: The mucosa and wall of the esophagus intact and gray-pink, without lesions or injuries. Approximately 125 ml of partially digested semisolid food is found in digestive tract. *Urinary System*: Kidneys are anatomic in size, shape and location and without lesions. *Male Genital System*: Structures are within typical limits. Evidence of recent sexual activity but no indication activity was anything other than normal. Urethral fluid samples removed for analysis. *Toxicology/Serology*: Sample of pleural blood and bile submitted for toxicological analysis, stomach contents saved. Fourteen (14) autopsy photographs and three (3) postmortem x-rays have been itemized, catalogued and processed according to procedure, chain of custody strictly adhered to throughout, personal effects sent to central lab for further analysis.

CRIMINAL INVESTIGATIVE ANALYSIS. PRELIMINARY ASSESSMENT. EXCERPT. Behavioral Analysis Unit 2, Federal Bureau of Investigation, Southwest Division. The people who occupied the other half of the duplex the victim rented seem to have been away for the evening. No one heard a thing, no sign of break-in. Suspect seems to have walked in through an unlocked door. ... Note the bruises across the knuckles: consistent with some sort of struggle. But, as you can see from the next slide, they are also consistent with the victim striking his hand against the bathroom mirror. Possibly a missed punch. Note the splatter pattern on the mirror and the glass in the sink. ...There are, as was stated earlier, broken ribs suggestive of something other than metal. The ruined nose and bruised knees seem to have been caused when the victim struck the marble floor after being hit from behind. Typical law of exchange: he struck the ground hard, and the ground struck back. No fingerprints, no hair fibers, no DNA at either the initial scene of violence or anywhere in the house. The assault seems to have been exquisitely planned. Traces of blood around the inside rim of drain pan and copper tubing are the victim's. Otherwise, there is little evidence of primary or secondary transfer. Nonetheless, and this is no mere conjecture on our part, we doubt we will find much in terms of further trace evidence, other than what the investigation team leaves behind. We have a serial killer on our hands, gentlemen. The bastard is good. Members of LAPD's Special Serial Killer Ad Hoc Task Force have their own copy.

∞

My father, he typed distractedly, unable to fall asleep, the bottle of scotch empty beside him, had the makings of a great man, despite what people said. But he was a particular kind of failure, going as far as he could and floundering there, until the middle distance was all he could see, all he could accomplish. He had one overriding scruple: he wanted us to be happy. For the most part we were (my sisters included). In the 70s he brought us back from a failed stint as missionaries in the Dominican Republic to settle here where he worked for the same insurance company twenty-odd years. When he spoke Spanish to potential converts in *Hoyos del Corazón,* somewhere south or southwest of the Cordillera Central, he did it with British undertones, an affectation he had picked up on his way to our first and only mission trip abroad, thinking it made him sound cultured. Being civilized was, as far as I can tell, his entire view of salvation. Fall in love with the time and place you live in, he once told me, and when you move, take it with you like a piece of luggage. It pays to be mercilessly aware, he said. It matters little that it mattered, he said, it matters that you cared. We understood half the things he said, listened mostly to the voice, an echo of my grandmother's, fluid if not a little cranky. You have the eyes of a sea turtle, he told me another time; I bet you could swim your way through a sea of salt. He meant it as a compliment, I suppose, but I spent nights with a flashlight beneath the covers, studying my hands, and I developed an aversion to sodium chloride. Later he would take me up on his lap and squeeze my legs, below and above the kneecaps. You have the legs of a donkey; don't trade them in for

144

anything; they'll help you on your long climb up. Why would he do that? Why leave a kid to question his own nature? One New Year's Eve, at the stroke of midnight or thereabouts, he walked into the room I shared with my own growing self. I was awake, earphones on, listening to Alvin Lee wail on his monster guitar. I had my back toward the door, eyes closed, holding myself at a near frenzy, slipping deeper and deeper into that wall of sound. But someone else was inside the room with me! I opened my eyes and turned. I think he meant to hug me. I winced and backed away. He put his hands up, to show me they were empty. Sorry, he said, sorry. Words, no sound (my earphones were on), a gesture at something. He backed out of the room. I took off my earphones and snuck to the door. I could hear him mumbling to my mother, hurt in places I didn't know a man his age or experience could hurt. I didn't know what to do? didn't know what I was supposed to have felt or how to respond? I backed into my room, put the earphones on, and turned the music up louder. A day later I found a letter addressed to me on my bed.

Son,

We live always in the stretch or sag of our nerves, either on the crest or in the trough of feeling. This impotency is bitter to us, and makes us live only for the seen horizon, reckless what spite we inflict or endure. We learn that there are pangs too sharp, griefs too deep, ecstasies too high for our finite selves to register. When emotions reach this pitch the mind chokes; and memory goes white till circumstances are humdrum once more.

Your father

I read the letter over and over again, thinking, how could I have misjudged him? how could I have failed him? And punished myself because I knew I would never be able to live up to him. Sometime during my last year of post-graduate work, I realized he'd copied, with a change in tenses, parts of Lawrence's introduction to *Seven Pillars of Wisdom*. I was livid. He'd stolen the only thing I thought his. What a sad fuck. He failed me as he had failed himself, climbing the wall of paternal love on someone else's back. He must have been desperate. He must have known I'd eventually figure it out. I always wondered if he lived long enough to realize he'd cheated himself of a real moment.

∞

The Younger Detective. The older detective's partner stood on the decking of the first floor and looked out toward the hillside. Late summer, middle of the month, feeling out of control. The backyard, dropping down and off yards from the back of the house, lapped at the rim of a ravine running lengthwise against granite hills. There were trees with branches sticking up from the crown of their tops and shorter ones with branches spread out as if to catch the wind. Those over there rustled, those farther out provided shade. He fingered a cigarette. His partner, the older detective, was somewhere in the house, peering into corners, the up and downside of things. He couldn't help him there; he hadn't really known her; he'd only get in the way. Why had she been such a bitch about everything? His questions had been, on the whole, not that dumb. He understood things, things he could have taught her, things they could have shared. No one should have to die alone. Her killer must have...— hell, who knew why he'd picked her, any of them. But why, why her? Was he that out of control? Was he trying to send a message? Or merely a master of the taunt? The younger detective tossed the cigarette into the bushes and the pack in after it. He existed in a world of his own making, where trees,

146

forensic pathologists and serial killers, had a purpose and function but no name. Why couldn't he remember her name? Would she have remembered his? He tried to remember the name on the lab coat she wore the first time he'd met her, first autopsy, the body count about to tick up. Why hadn't he committed it to memory? *He* had a name, didn't he? Had he told her, whispered it, tortured her with it, let her die with it on the curve of her ear? What torment or knowledge did it finally bring? I need a name, you bastard, I need a name.

∞

Maybe it was the age or the times they were living in. Or the city. *Zoon politikon.* Man, the political animal. And something else, something about the complex web of relations that, when multiplied exponentially, linked everyone to everyone else. He'd read about that somewhere (hadn't he?) in a book about...— what was it? Cities in general or this particular city, the last of the last frontiers — arid, windblown, floundering from a deficiency of design, and row upon row of the sameness of intention. Here and there, pocketed in borrowed facts and suspicious sentences, he recognized, or thought he did, aspects of the life around him, semblances, throwaway correspondences, portraits proximate and remote, but not much else. Dystopia. He recalled the word suddenly ... but what else? Fragments, lost residues, a minefield of words, in a head full of the misplaced and mismatched. He chose that moment to open his eyes. The curtains were drawn. That he had dreamed was a possibility, that the dream had crooned prospects and options to his reptilian brain for safe keeping yet another, that that one word, inflicting itself into consciousness like a circus barker, was the tag end of an opening into nothing, was a damned shame or an invited mystery. Sunday, he believed it was Sunday, had to be Sunday, for no other reason than he had arrived on Thursday, three days from. His pajama legs had ridden up almost to the bottom of his knees somewhere around three or four o'clock in the morning, ghost hours, specter and anticipation. They were supposed to be static proof; they were supposed to be cotton-weight flannel; they were supposed to ride cleanly and warmly against the tops of his feet all night long for however long. Couldn't anyone get anything right? Someone had written a poem about Sunday mornings, he remembered that much; the year of our Lord two thousand twelve, somebody had to have written something. A poem, a song, a prayer for forgiveness. Get up you fool, get up, no one's going to do it for you. He was supposed to be goofing and basking and killing time. He almost laughed at that. He'd been gifted with something of might by a power he never knew existed until it had taken possession of him years ago and had grown, branch and limb, like a well-watered tree. The ability to reach out, in a gesture he imagined ultimately welcoming, and effortlessly cut one lonely cord in that complex web of relations. A beneficence of some kind, he believed, when he let himself believe anything at all. Yes, I'm listening, and, yes, I see you. I do. He had learned to listen, taught himself to care. He did laugh.

∞

Special Agent Eden Stuart Traherne, Federal Bureau of Investigation, Criminal Investigations, Southwest Division. Special Agent Eden Stuart Traherne had a theory, portions of which were subject to conjecture. The vanishing point was invented or discovered, depending on which source you read, and she had read them all, by Donatello, da Vinci, Perugino, Brunelleschi or Masaccio, more or less at about the same time. Good enough and well said. In the end nevertheless neither the Renaissance nor the Italian quattrocento painters, however canonical, ever mattered in her theory. She was less interested to be honest in the vanishing point in and of itself than in the perspectives it engendered. Linear, curvilinear, reverse. Certain crucial artists in certain crucial centuries drew on each of these perspectives for certain crucial works of art. Nonetheless, she had set aside, for the sake of her theory and its coherence, the first and last of these to concentrate on the second: to the mapping of five vanishing points into a circle, with four of them at cardinal headings N, W, S, E, the final one at the circle's origin. As a result, Special Agent Eden Stuart Traherne had managed, out of instinct perhaps, more likely sheer grind, to plot the unsub's kills from their supposed beginning to their near end to the north, west and south portions of the city. Nothing in the east. Not yet. The unsub was, for all intents and purposes, planning his next move, his next performance if you will, similar signature, similar design, somewhere in the east of the city. (What else could he be doing?) And when that happened, Special Agent Eden Stuart Traherne would reverse-engineer the lines of convergence, and graph them back to where the kills originated, the center of the circle. She would have her killer. A good theory, a working theory. Chains of reasoning, justified belief. It was either that or she had her head completely up her ass. She just had to wait.

∞

He noticed a hesitancy in the air, the day and its rhythms like briefly held notes, and against treetops and skyline an accumulation of clouds. His car was where he'd left it. But why should that surprise him? He hadn't moved it in at least three days. *Grazioso*. He hoped it had something to do with the day. (He read so much and remembered so little. He knew people who could recite whole verses of poetry with little urging or spout

149

sports statistics in a jocular vein. Most of the time he was teased to distraction by all the words he'd stuffed in his head.) Midway through his walk was a stretch of plants, trees, overgrowth and offshoot, grown out of plan: a primeval vengeance, planted and forgotten long ago, reaching for open sky, grasping empty air and car fumes instead. The leaf of a dying plant swayed briefly in the wind, as if propelled by a tiny invisible hand. Going through he felt a special thrill, as if something, someone, would jump out of the shadows and grab at his throat. He came upon a boy on a stoop, hands wild in the air, mocking the wind. The boy stopped abruptly as he passed by and ran toward the back of the house. He smiled up at the boy but the boy was gone. He regretted that, walking in on someone else's dream, waking them up.

He walked leisurely, taking in the sights, the street stretching past the horizon. On one block a house was being built, skeletal walls exposed to the sun; on another a wall of soaring hedges obscured everything but the top of a dusk-colored chimney. Boys chasing a dog could be heard through the curtain of green. Past that, stood a house he could only describe as Moroccan Baroque. The sidewalk narrowed. A squirrel scurried up a tree, stopped to eye him for a moment, its head slightly cocked to one side, and blinked, once, twice, three or four times more had he stuck around to count. Cars whipped past him. He passed a house with window boxes agleam with morning glories, jonquils, columbines, trumpet vine. He smiled at the world, suddenly happy, and picked up his pace. He was beginning to feel like a character in a story, and beginning to like it. In the story the day was much like today, an April wind against cooling skin. There was comfort in that. The sidewalk opened up again. Houses and more houses, each one different than the rest. Finally, a two-story craftsman-style beauty in powder blue and pale trim. An airy porch on one side, on the other a set of mullioned windows through which he glimpsed a wall of books lovingly in place.

"She's amazing, isn't she?" Faded blue jeans, beach sandals, t-shirt with a red swirl at the breast, face and arms tanned. Mid-forties if he had to guess.

"Yours?"

"No, but I wish she was," voice wistful. "I live down the street. I like to imagine myself walking downstairs to pick up the morning newspaper and seeing people staring at my house. I've always wanted a house other people could admire, and this one's a beaut." The man was talking to himself now, forgetting there was someone he'd stopped to talk to. "I think it has to do with line and scale. She's meant to belong here and the landscape grew around her as a compliment."

Nice image, he thought, trying to put himself in the man's place.

"Where are my manners," the man said, interrupting himself. "William," extending a hand. "Yours?"

"It depends."

William gave him a quizzical glance.

"My parents use one name," he said, "my siblings another. The safest would be Junior — although it's been awhile since I've felt that young."

William laughed as he would with a friend. "My older brother got saddled with that one. Thank God."

"First boy, after two sisters. Guess I had no choice." It was always easier to start out with the truth, however misleading, than to invent something he might have to take back. They went back to looking at the house. "Can I ask you something?"

"Sure."

151

"Why are houses 'she'?"

"Don't know." William's brow furrowed. "I don't think you can say 'He's a beauty' to describe a house — a horse maybe, but never a house."

"Unless he's a filly." Both smiling now.

"I think it has to do with the domestic being a woman's domain." William shook his head. "If my wife heard me saying that she'd kill me. But it's true, don't you think?"

"Boats are feminine too, aren't they?"

"Right, right."

"Because they're commanded by men."

"I'm going to let that one go. I'm in enough trouble as it is."

Men of William's unquestioning camaraderie made the easiest targets. There was so little to appeal to; they brought that to the table themselves; you hardly had to strain to produce the allure.

"From across the street you can see that it sweeps back just so, every angle perfectly executed," William continued. "See how the windows receive the sun at the right slant for maximum light. Even the cobblestone walkway to the porch, which if you didn't know any better might seem like an afterthought, but it's dictated by the placement of the house. As you walk up you have to face her the way she wants you to, dead-on, her best features toward you."

"You an architect or something?"

"An admirer of beauty, and I guess I'm a little obsessed. I'm sorry, am I keeping you from somewhere?"

"Out for a walk. This is as good a place as any to stop."

"Ah," going back to his reverie. "The other houses on the street were built for show, but this one — "

"Form and function."

"Exactly. Beats everything every time."

"Aren't these kinds of houses supposed to be painted darker colors?"

"Probably, but it's a good choice, don't you think? As if heralding the view."

He was enjoying himself now, outside his own claustrophobic sense of things.

"If you go around the back there's a pergola that acts as a garage with the same lines and proportions in miniature."

"Do you think it's deliberate?" thinking out loud. "How do people know the ideas in their heads will materialize the way they envisioned?"

William chuckled. "That's what makes them artists and us poor slubs."

He smiled, toying with the idea of being a slub.

William called attention to the attic's construction, how the collar beams spanning the rafters front to back did most of the work, something about ceiling joists, horizontal members, decorative braces, and much else, he'd stopped trying to follow the words, they meant nothing of themselves, but the tone of voice wedged itself in his ear, a quality of speech bordering on the reverential. There was a sense of being introduced to a mystery, if not of life in general then of the human heart. He despised mysteries; he was going to have to punish William for his.

"I'm going on, aren't I?"

"Not at all. It's good to hear someone enthusiastic about something other than themselves."

"You shouldn't be so hard on people," William shook his head and put a hand on his shoulder. "We're all doing the best we can."

Normally he couldn't abide being touched, much less by a

stranger, but there was something heartening about the weight of the hand. It was felt as a real loss when it was pulled away.

"I should get back to my wife. She's become quite jealous of this old gal. Nice meeting you, enjoy your walk."

"I will, thanks."

"Loosen up, life'll be a lot better if you do," William said, starting to walk away. "And listen, next time you're around, drop by. I'm at the corner over there. Me, the wife and the four girls."

"Four?"

"Unbelievable, I know," lingering briefly, glad to be outdoors in the company of another man.

"Your wife won't mind?"

"As long as we don't spend too much time talking about the house, she won't." William was near the corner and the light was about to turn green. "Anytime, right."

He waived back and turned to the house. People could be seen stirring about and feeling that he was intruding he started off.

∞

CRIMINAL INVESTIGATIVE ANALYSIS. PRELIMINARY ASSESSMENT. EXCERPT. Behavioral Analysis Unit 2, Federal Bureau of Investigation, Southwest Division. Of greater interest is the following excerpt from a letter, verbatim, unsigned, found on the victim's laptop, written, we believe, some time prior to his death (a fuller, encrypted version follows). Unit specialists are working to see if they can scare up any trace of tampering. If the metadata on the laptop's internal logs has been doctored this might tell us something about who we are dealing with. More to the point: We now have something concrete to go on, something that will help us understand, to the extent we can, the killer's mindset. The operational profile based on the entire text is attached. No one here, as stated earlier, believes the document was written by the victim himself — although his are the only fingerprints on the laptop. The bindings were not as tightly fastened as on some of the other victims, and further analysis will have to be made to reject the possibility the puncture wound was self-inflicted. That said, there is no way, logistically, the victim could have bled to death, typed the letter, and subsequently cleaned up the crime scene. Unless, of course, the killer had an accomplice, someone as yet identified. If this is the case, we have a bigger problem on our hands. How and to what extent depends on further analysis.

'Father,

'I've discovered I no longer need my name. I am an attitude, an approach, a development for others to misconstrue or hide behind. They'll try father, won't they? But they won't succeed. ... The sun outside is warm, father. Clouds provoke what there is of the shapeless light; nothing else quite seems to get the job done. ... Tell me father, do you think my life would have turned out differently if I'd learned to be an unrivaled potter at his wheel rather than who I am? I, myself, as you know, am a work of many hands, my own included. Have I fulfilled your promise, father? ... We never did have the same language, you and I, but you're all I have now, not because other things are beyond me father but because nothing is. In that department I can say I've overachieved.

Yours truly'

∞

He walked back the way he had come, the angles and sharp

lines of the house still in his head. Past the neighborhood drug store, he ran into an emaciated old man, black as pitch, a fine carpet of tight white curls adorning his head. He was holding a greasy hand-lettered sign "Poems for a nickel" and smiling encouragingly at everyone who passed by. The smell coming off the man reminded him of turnips, earthy and blunt. His clothes were threadbare but remarkably clean, the fingernails on his hands so fair they looked polished. What the hell, it was only a nickel. The poem was two pages long, the words "No color but clearness" like an incantation at the end of each verse. The words sounded familiar. "Is this yours?" turning back to the old man.

"Not anymore, young man, not anymore. You just bought it." He was taking out more pages from a knapsack, getting ready for his next customer.

"I mean did you write this — it's fairly good?"

"Maybe, maybe not, does it matter if it makes you happy?"

"I suppose."

"Yes, well, most people do. Look son, it's not always important to be the first with something, 'slong as you know what to do with what you got." The old man's smile displayed impossibly even white teeth, gums chocolate brown. He wasn't sure if he was being made fun of. "Smile, boy, smile. You'd have thought you lost your shoes in the war."

He shook his head, taking a quarter out of his pocket.

"Sorry, son, but I'm in bidness. One poem, one nickel. Anything else would make me a beggin' man."

"All right then, I'll take five more."

"Can't do that — what would my other customers say?" He began arranging pieces of paper on a rise of decorative concrete in front of a bank. "Half a day to go, can't be turning down my regulars, can I?"

"Think of it as an honorarium."

"I know that one, but I'm far too young, and not dressed for it. Not today, not today."

"Can I come back tomorrow?"

"I'll be here. Not too hard to miss. Ole man Rollo, that's me."

He started to walk away.

"Wait. Got me something here for you," diving into his knapsack. "Give it to your sweetheart, bring her a smile."

He took the piece of paper. The writing was just as neat and precise as before, ceremonial on the wrinkled page, not one word misspelled.

Tablet of Values

Swift bracing air
a moment of solitude,
and the mind's fleet currents.
Look, the city is laid bare,
and the passion for seeing has
lost its stern meaning.
Anywhere else I would have been lost, too,
but here I succumb to the silence,
the smile of trees, wet in their bending —
what good is the diplomacy of things
if interrogated for their worth?
Yellow slickers when it rains,
Buttons on bright shirts,
and the sun's ritual beaming.
In autumn and spring it's just you.

The words evoked a feeling of peacefulness, something to do with the smile of trees and the diplomacy of things being interrogated. He had owned a yellow rain slicker when he was about eight. His uncle had bought it for him. He'd been happy then. The old man was going to have to pay for that.

A powder-blue house and a tablet of values: two gifts in one day. He didn't have a sweetheart to give the poem to, but it didn't matter, someday he would. He thought of himself sitting on a corner somewhere, old as history, handing out poems to passersby for a nickel. He'd be a street bard of no little renown, no one paying attention to who he was. He laughed out loud. Two gifts in one day, William and the old man, alive to the nuances of life, each in his own way and without apology. Would he kill William's wife and his four daughters as a nuisance or because he could?

∞

The Older Detective. He wandered from room to room, floor to floor, careful not to plan his next move, careful to let chance and interest dictate turn and return. Eventually he found himself next to the wall unit. Swimmers and loungers, tropical from the look of them. Impenetrable glass. He tapped a finger at it. Notable workmanship; the thing would last a lifetime.

"You. Help me out here."

"I'm quite busy over here."

"Let's not make a twelve-year marriage out of this."

"I'm here, I'm here."

"See there."

"I don't see a thing."

"Look again."

"Manufacturer's brand. Is that why you called me over?"

The older detective scowled heavily. "Look again." Would

have bristled, had he known how.

The evidence technician stooped to take a closer look.

"What's that on the pupils, what would be the pupils?"

"Crosshairs, if I'm not mistaken."

"Someone's playing a joke."

Like a Hallmark card addressed to your wife, but not from you. Or a free trip all expenses paid to the capital of Kyrgyzstan instead of the capital of France.

The older detective wouldn't get the makings of the joke until days later.

"A partial print. With the usual distortions. But good enough to get a passably good match. The cleaning lady's."

"The cleaning lady's?"

"The cleaning lady's."

"But how did she ...?"

"We're trying to contrive the means. And how that decal, or whatever it is, made its way inside the fish tank to begin with. The working premise is that it was added at point of shipment or point of delivery and installation. Interviews with people responsible for any of these actions led to dead ends. None of them fit the profile."

"They never do."

"Never do what detective?"

"Fit the profile ... until they do. By then it's a different profile."

∞

ὁ θεὸς ἀγάπη ἐστίν. God they tell us, God is love. What a temptation. Thursday afternoon, yet again, the Dow Jones is up and the murder rate's flattened out. The local news has taken to clips of stray dogs and wandering bears in hillside neighborhoods. Well at least the news from Spain hasn't gotten worse. I read once — yes, that's me, the proverbial page turner, a hoarder of words, reader manqué — I read once that horses with broken legs are shot while men with broken souls write through the night. A bit dramatic, don't you think? But here I sit, writing through the night while everyone else slumbers. And what of that poor horse, weren't his legs, like our souls, something essential, speed against the wind, the force that propelled it through bound and leap, gallop and rapture? But you came looking for answers, clarification and account. Read on, dear reader, read on, maybe something will turn up. You shouldn't kid young children — they always laugh at the joke not realizing it was made at their expense. Hush little baby, don't say a word, mama's gonna buy you a mockingbird. And if that mockingbird won't sing, mama's gonna buy you a diamond ring. Old folk are a different problem: they keep waiting for the joke to end so they can hear it again. The lesson here is that at either end of the spectrum dependable outcomes are never guaranteed. I have a friend who can't deal with paragraphs longer than two or three sentences, newspaper style. Can't scan them, can't digest them, not even a bite at a time. Flips pages to find dialogue. Even here length soon becomes an issue. Declarative statements work best. Must be difficult to deal with circumstances where ambiguity and deep meaning are at play. Is it cheeky or charming, to say I've said nothing, told you nothing, will tell you nothing? Should I plead love or forbearance? Read on dear reader, read on.

∞

The Odd Couple. They died happy, content, spanning more than a century between them, each just this or that side of fifty at time of death. They met at a transformational seminar, a brief history of everything, archetypal and all that, the long swing of coastline Mediterranean if one blinked past the fact, dolphins on the horizon no one thought had been leased on short

160

notice and shipped back. Redemption was in the air, deliverance perhaps, some sort of starting over. She was an East Coast transplant, too brisk, too knowing, the speed of her speech razor-sharp and penetrating, even when she was wrong, he a Texan who'd lost his south-Lubbock twang somewhere on the road from Van Horn, TX to Ehrenberg, AZ, 697.46 miles in either direction. Both, as it turns out, two days into the weekend, in perfected bliss. She fell in love with his ears, what passed for a beard, and the full shock of him; he with her pleasurable mouth, edges less wounding once he understood the cuts would eventually heal, and then of course her shapely acquiescent breasts. Dated for five months, married on the sixth, honeymooned in Santa Barbara, at a seaside resort with semi-detached cabanas, miniature tiki torches for sale, aloha shirts to match, moved to Woodland Hills, south of the boulevard of course, 50s ranch-style home, kids' dream, fruit trees, swimming pool, parking for guests, lovely block of houses, quiet neighborhood. Found, like the Andreases, in a basement crawlway, heads together, self-effacing, ancient-looking as the kings of Persia, beaming as though tickled by a German lullaby. Survived by three sisters on her side, a gay older brother and a mother on his, outraged they had moved away from familiar surroundings, their place in the world, had moved without hesitation, without fear or favor, to the end of some kind of line and the beginning of another. That year they would have vacationed in Egypt. Or maybe Japan?

The Walker. She had made it this far on the promise of a decent paying job but had begun taking long evening walks to postpone the fact dinner was eaten alone. Hers was a corner studio she'd turned into office, living room, bedroom, library, kitchen, dining area, cloak room, attic. Lovely womanish baritone, second F below middle C, her diction essentially impeccable. The neighbors were nice enough, except for the man across the stunted courtyard, darting naked room to room as though chasing after himself, blinds open, forgetting that civilization had invented privacy as an act of even exchange. Her heart gave way, her sense of innocence and fair play, when someone complained to the manager she smoked too much. She'd been promised a raise by the end of the year, and another the year after. She was going to save up and move into a real apartment as soon as she could. She expected people to look her in the eye on her evening walks and was startled by their discomfort or sheer umbrage. The night has a smile on her face, her mother would say, half poet, half holy fool. Where I grew up, her mother would say, we named our dogs after features of the landscape. Her father would turn the afternoon paper to the business page. Americans, her mother would say, name their dogs after former friends, and tap on the dishwasher as if to hurry the rinse cycle. Wouldn't it be easier to pick up the phone and apologize? Your mother's from the old country, her father would say, and gesture north and eastward. Where, she had been taught, if she remembered correctly, the state of New York was located. Don't talk to strangers, her mother would say. Allow yourself never to be that raw or naive. She hardly knew how to respond. In any case, she had been a child then, she was an adult now. She would do as she pleased.

The city at night, less than you expected, more than you anticipated. Streetlights flickered, palm trees preened, noises carried. Somewhere ahead or behind her a siren squealed. Around the next corner a car alarm whined. In the distance an unbroken low electric hum, as though the city, buildings tall and empty, was trying to croon itself to sleep. The occasional bus, driver nodding at the wheel, sped by in the opposite direction. Fog rolled in off the coast. June gloom. Funny, despite all, she didn't feel gloomy. Her body was discovered, light as a moonbeam, unassuming as dreamless sleep, somewhat starting to stink, somewhat starting to bloat, by an honest enough squatter (who had briefly thought of moving on to more welcoming quarters) in for the night in an abandoned apartment complex half completed, half left to rot.

Mr. Mister. He was actually shorter than most men he knew, but with near perfect proportions people rarely suspected he was only so tall. Lived just shy of the Miracle Mile. The neighborhood kids had called him Mr. Mister for as long as he could remember; so long in fact he sometimes had difficulty remembering his name, something vaguely Middle-European, consonants edging out vowels three to one. A bit jowly at any age, the extra flesh occasionally spoiling looks and demeanor, but not for long, there were grace notes in the way he walked. Not surprisingly, he loved kids and dogs and the infrequent cat. He had learned to pitch his voice to the balconies, although he was in the wrong city for that.

"Where you going today, Mr. Mister?"

"To the museum to see if they've dug up any new bones. Would you like to come?"

"I don't think my mother would like me hanging around dirty old bones a nasty old dog dug up."

"She would if she could see the dog that dug these up."

"You just making that up."

"Let her know I'll be going back there again in a couple of weeks. Should be enough time for her to come around."

Child and man walked off in different directions, happy as the world was round.

"Turn around."

"Look, let's talk this out."

"I said turn around."

"Why?"

"As an exclamation can be used to add emphasis to a response."

"Please ..."

"I think you should let that one go."

"Please."

"Turn around."

"This is insane."

"There's an outside chance."

"But why? No, I mean it. Why? What could you possibly get out of this?"

"It's what I do. It's who I am."

Years later, the boy, mostly grown and subject to rumination, would think of Mr. Mister and wonder where oh where had the dogs of the city buried his bones?

The Kid. "I'm afraid it's time for me to go back to work."

"I interrupted your lunch, didn't I? You probably wanted the time to yourself? You're onto something." The kid pointed at the opened laptop. "And I'm ... intruding or something."

"You should stop apologizing," lightly placing his hand over the kid's for a second, bringing color to his face. "Everything's fine."

"Sorry, sorry. I mean ... ah ..."

Dark unkempt hair and the flashing of teeth, contemporary as so many his age (early twenties?) in clothes not altogether clean or well-laundered, eyes betraying a kind of blushing insistence. Not bad-looking, if you liked the type, and were of his inclination. Didn't matter. In the sport he was in, sexual preference was of little importance; he had learned long ago that any appetite could be turned to advantage.

"Not a problem. We could do this again, if you'd like?

"That would be great. I mean ... You wouldn't mind?"

"Not at all." If the kid had been looking for someone older to take matters into his own hands, he couldn't have picked a better candidate.

"Great, great, I have a business card here somewhere. I don't really have ... I mean, not what you'd call ... But never mind that. I'll just write my cell phone number on the back. That should work, shouldn't it?"

"We could go to a game. Fly-fishing. Parasailing. Or we could just hang out."

"Fly-fishing? Parasailing? A game?" As though translating back from a dead language.

They shook hands. What else were they supposed to do? He had almost run after the kid, the way he had tilted his head, brokenly, as he'd walked away.

An opening gambit, that's all this was. Stratagems, schemes, depth and dimension, feints and counter-feints, the entire parade of outlines, rundowns, final plans. Before or after dinner, economy of means or slow torture? The devil was in the details. Afterwards, he'd relax for a year or two; he owed himself that much. The desert perhaps, inland perhaps, lands unknown, reasons unknown. The air was bracing with a subtle trusting breeze and one or two lost bees round the corner and to the right, the trees guarding the distance like sentries looking forward to the medals they forgot to collect the first time around. Had he possessed a romantic temperament he would have labeled the color on the horizon *bleu céleste*. He wished he knew how to whistle or sing a perfect tune. It seemed to him the day, the landscape of promise and bliss, required a sponsoring theme. Such joy should reverberate, should echo and ring. Strategy and tactics, tactics and strategy, he would have to balance these against an expansiveness he felt would swallow him up if he wasn't careful. He said hello to everyone he passed, to hear the sound of his own mounting glee.

Fugitive Dust

The two-lane road leads east and inland through pasture and scrub grass, the occasional cow in the distance like a mote in someone else's eye. The wedding is that side of an eighty-mile stretch of dun fields and denuded hillsides. Eventually you have to cut north and into a sweep of scarcely arable land people punish themselves year after year to tease into life. Green is a miracle color and any yield a miracle crop. Generations of families give birth here, marry and remarry, discovering and rediscovering why marriage, a crucible of sorts all things considered, is such a godsend after all: Mormon-recruiting territory, with thoughts of bringing back blue laws. I may be exaggerating, making the whole thing up. Long stretches of road without a rest stop and an overactive bladder will do that to you. And the color of place. The San Joaquin Valley: Fresno, Kern, San Joaquin County, Madera, Merced, Tulare, Stanislaus, Waterford, Corcoran, Lost Hills. Bureaucrats, I kid you not, dub the place an "eight-hour nonattainment area". Something to do with "the accumulations of carbon monoxide, ground-level ozone (1-hour), particulate matter (PM-10), sulfur dioxide, multiple exceedance days, stagnant air masses, fermenting cattle feed, entrained outflows of sulfates, nitrates, vinyl chloride, volatile organic compounds, stagnant weather patterns, lack of precipitation and high temperatures, fugitive dust and on-road mobile vehicle exhaust, and the non-availability of reasonably available control measures (RACM)". Sardonic bastards. So here we are on an eight-hour nonattainment zone on our way to see my niece marry one of the Valley's native sons, whom we've yet to meet, not face-to-face in any case, from a long line of nonattainment men — he cashiered himself from the army after failing the Army Engineer Officer Advance Course three times in two months, something to do with backbreaking experience forms and an equally backbreaking application processes, and his father and grandfather had failed at farming in a place where failure is a given ("violent crime 24% higher, access to healthcare 31% lower, college attendance consistently 50% below average, average per capita incomes 32.2% lower and unemployment rates four to eight points higher than the state's"), the latter going on to star in one of several local mariachi bands, touring status unknown, the former landing a job as a prison guard at Avenal, Delano, Wasco, somewhere. So here we are, out past stretches of lonely hills and the build-up of carbon monoxide, ground-level ozone, fermenting cattle feed, volatile organic compounds, fugitive dust, and the lack of reasonably available control measures, headed, inevitably, nonattainably, north and further east, toward Madera, principal city of the Madera–Chowchilla Metropolitan Statistical Area, the county seat of Madera County, where all things green and fresh and tender are thinking of jumping ship. I'm exaggerating again. Only by so much. There is, however, plenty of sunshine, the wettest year that of 1983.

I've talked to him on the phone a few times. He has the

oddest speech impediment, not consistent, not easily discernible, until the ear catches up. Globs, he said. In a meandering speech about dress uniforms. The "v" a "b", the "e" dangling from the roof of his mouth but never dropping off, the "s" like a short intemperate hiss thrown back by the wind. He says "sojers" for soldiers. Duck tape. Let's flush this out. Bob wire. Chester drawers. His favorite past time? Refurnishing furniture. Old-timers disease (okay, I'll give him that one). Perhaps it's not a speech impediment; perhaps no one's ever taught his tongue how to form certain sounds or the meaning of words. Perhaps it's something else, perhaps I lack an ear for nuance. Seems like a fine fellow otherwise, having served in the military, honorably, through two tours and a reserve posting, and loves my niece more than anyone else I know. I hope she'll be happy. I do.

Pudding

Slow. Fast. Slow, fast. Slowfast. Slowfast, Slowfast, Slowfast the III, second heir, second marriage, third wife, was a tall and simple man, the stature doesn't matter, the modesty does, whose effortlessness and charm ran in either direction, both of which, one could say, were disqualifying and miscalculated, but then one didn't understand the man. He held entitlements and emoluments from an ancestry hoary and Christian in all their accoutrements and pious undertakings, the former enfilading the latter, the latter serving cover for the last, as any would-be Pope would find hard to match, he of course would oblige and seat them to his right on occasions petty and seigneurial or any otherwise prepossessing repast, accompanied in all his offices and remonstrances by so serene and premeditated a personage as the Duchess von fitzDuckwild. She suffered from migraines. It was a history without a past and mostly through the occipital nerve. It also made her a candidate for gout. In junior years and trips abroad it was an occasion for fright and distant memories. The memories were of John Erstwhile, whom she'd never met but would have willingly succumbed to such early knowledge as would have been his birthright to command. He died too early and much too young. She on the other hand scaled age as any other anonymously and overwhelmingly exhausted mountain if only for the pure pleasure of it and in August if no other month. It allowed her servants, and one or two grandchildren, to underscore the sagacity of her skates across a vastness of freedom and ice and leave no mark or the shape of any wild thing fool enough to follow, shadow or no shadow, meat on the bone or mere gristle. There were six of them, the grandchildren. One of whom word world whirl.

"Gran, are you pretty?"

"Women of a certain age can be said to have falsified it, wouldn't have any sense apart from that. In twenty more years I can have. Only in the company of modifying women, however. Men, men, men. Men!" She sighed deeply. In her bosom and in her chest. "You heard it here first."

Her granddaughter leered and fled, petticoats flying, in pink and cherry blossoms. It would do no good to maintain, and then of course the parse. Gran was always right. Men! And of course it was Summer, one couldn't argue with the clock, it was in all its turnings (although Gran did, argue, with the clock, Summer, but she did, twice a day sometimes, never on a Monday or a Tuesday or a Wednesday or a Thursday or a Friday or a Saturday or blessed Sunday, but most days, however half, especially if milk and proper breeding were involved). Gosh, I think I'm saying too much, aren't I? Nevertheless, you did ask.

"Are we fried yet?" Slowfast, calling from the library. (I have mentioned Slowfast, haven't I? It's not too late to beseech thee in its proper form, if he's to be involved, that is?)

Someone answered, but the man was outside milking Barbary Coast, who was suffering insomnia very badly, and in grief that its dreams, stalled and bale, were over there in Ireland and the visa innocent of stamps, and the answer echoed across Japan and Southern parts, somebody must have heard it, but it wasn't Slowfast, having the worst of it, and not yet misunderstood. Have a wallop at it.

Becky, Becky, Becky. She was grand. Announce it next Tuesday. Apple streusel eyes and a nose no one should do without; you could see at a distance and know beforehand how the day turned out; it was a thing to remember but without the intended data, it was that much more or less. Like Caesar's wife. If only her other cast members would agree. Rebecca Darlington Markham, what a romance. The fundamental question is this. He'd gotten the initials right.

Wir setzen an dieser Stelle über den Fluss. He'd understood that once, a schoolboy prank or its aftermath. Only with proper moustaches. Of which Slowfast was very proud. Reading from verse eleven, chapter two. And the thing flowed and the heavens conjectured, and he proud, stately, jutting, independent, utterly disemboweled, felt he couldn't go on, not such worthwhile, such beauty in the written word, such enunciation, such perspicacity backwards, it didn't need translation. Precisely, because he did not. In an atmosphere of want, the machinations full-throttled, the purpose thereof like a people in full senate above or below the line of scrimmage. Should I tell you what I know? Yes, here is where I'll start.

His hands looked competent enough. He was tall without having to show it and he had married well into a mood and a family with great wealth and a great pedigree going back at least some years. He vacationed in the capitals and skied in the Alps, took the sun in private in the summer territories and autumn where there was space to walk and the trees and the slight coming chill accompanying any stranger and none of them could have been any happier or marginally more delighted elsewhere perhaps and all for a good cause. He was going to get married (but I said that didn't I?) and it was a great adventure and a given fact and he was not altogether worried that he hadn't met the girl, it was a good contract, a decent appeal to luck, despite the codicils and the hedging back.

Perhaps a speech was in order. He recalled a grumble once. Or was it a groan? But that entailed a castle, architectural, epidemic, ignored, and too many characters to surmount, some who spoke in words and sentences but very little else. But his speech? In the American vernacular, in the American grain, soldiers and monuments and the future in verse. He confessed he never owned one. His father confessed, his mother confessed, his brother, a little sister he'd rarely met, people confessed. So many confessions, in concert, conjuntamente, de común acuerdo, but in whose language and which set of promises and misunderstandings, not a priest around, peripatetic, footloose, in the wrong town. Then there was the matter of limbs and branches: what's the purpose of a limb if not in its branches? The man in France would prance in a trance with a lance perchance to finance his budding romance in advance of mischance circumstance happenstance. But he had promised American, had promised in order. Siblings and strangers, weather and whether. A walk, a walk was in his future.

"Here Sparky, here. Good boy. Fetch once. We're here for hours, learn to pace and manage, manage and pace."

Partly real, partly dream-country, native trees and tall shrubs, white and red mulberry, black gum, Sparky was in for a surprise, where would he stop to sniff and rub and mark and have a preference if not a knack? He could be happy here. His

174

wife, when he picked one, likewise. What was I waiting for?

"Mrs. Makewell. Out on a stroll?"

"Mr. Slowfast. Out as well."

"A remarkable day, don't you think? The world is here, and our place in it. I was thinking pudding."

"Pudding? Yes."

"How's the husband?"

"How's the wife?"

"The possibility is altogether here once I'm done. She's a beauty, I understand. Never so than yesterday. Or the morrow. Have you met her? Is she nice?"

"Oh, Mr. Slowfast, you couldn't have picked a better day for it. Calm and assured as my Fred is bald, as the world is small, as worries are forever, and piano playing's a fad."

"I've been meaning to say something remarkably like that."

Sparky barked, unbelievably twice this time. Or was it Mrs. Makewell? Or someone farther back? Peacock feathers and the chance of sun.

"Mr. Slowfast."

"Mrs. Makewell."

"Why the proper British accent?"

"Should it be improper instead?"

"I don't think you understand the gravity of the thing, Mr. Slowfast."

"Gravity, yes, very important. It keeps you up at night."

The wind brayed and broke against the understanding of its nature.

"My turn, Mrs. Makewell."

"But only backwards, Mr. Slowfast."

"Tell me, Mrs. Makewell."

"Immediately, Mr. Slowfast."

"How long have we known each other?"

"Coming on too long, I'm afraid."

"And I trust you?"

"I wouldn't have it any other way."

"Right."

"Right."

"What country are we in?"

"The one it's always been, I'm afraid." She looked a little sad just then.

"And I'm happy here?"

"It would be an impertinence to say yes, Mr. Slowfast. However, it would be an impertinence to say no. Who decides?"

"Quite a puzzle."

"If you want to look at it that way."

"Which other way would there be?"

"Thousands, millions from the last count, millions upon millions. Country by country, state by state. Oh, my now, but I'm telling you what to do and it's your look. Mustn't push you beyond your limits, and beyond ours of course."

He looked out the window, right on cue. A beautiful day, the light aslant and persuasive, time to be outdoors and in sunshine, the clouds slow and kidding, you would immediately think rain, but it wasn't the season. The sound of surf outside. He remembered the word "car" without a prompt and the phrase four-oh-five. Still the sounds were alike, especially at night. He was beginning to tire, a small nap perhaps. If only they would last a little longer, he would be able to get the rest he wanted, the rest everyone promised.

"Ready for your treatment?"

"Ready."

"How's the journaling? Is it coming along?"

He brandished his laptop. Ten pages. He was very proud of himself; he was getting things under grasp.

The nurse agreed. Ten pages, what a triumph! He was on his way to a full recovery. The scars in the mirror didn't look so bad when you thought about it, when you put it into perspective. He was eating solid food now. Some. Soon he would recognize the face attached to the scars. Soon he would be able to walk the few steps to the bathroom unaided. Soon he would know who he was. Soon he would understand.

"Would you like me to burb it four times?" he said, gesturing with the laptop.

"Yes, of course, whatever you'd like. Let me finish adjusting this, then I'll take your vitals, enter them into the chart, and then you can start. I have a full half hour before my next patient."

The Troll's Tale

Once, in a faraway land — well, the San Fernando Valley, but no one crosses to that side of town unless you have to — in a place called Woodland Hills, there lived a troll who liked everything pickled or fried: shoes, belt buckles, thimbles, mail boxes, frog's legs, door jambs, sweet potatoes, asparagus, Swiss chard. The frying was done in walnut oil infused with a delicate inscrutable flavor. The pickling was done in brine every other Monday.

He'd never married — would you? (Marry a troll, I mean.) He's been known to carry off maidens and recalcitrant children, imprisoning them for life or palming them off to unsuspecting customers. (The police are baffled, editorials mount, and bloggers spot another trend.) Loves the written word, romance novels, test scores, door hangers, obituaries and Sunday morning cartoon puzzles. Knowledge is power, some people say (although where does it get them?). He simply has a taste for words, sweet, sour, astringent, doesn't matter their provenance.

His best friend's a toad, bearded, blushing with pride, semi-retired, with a failing belief he'll ever be called back to his stock-in-trade, selling encyclopedias door-to-door. He was the same generation as the troll, same set of values, same outlook on maidens and pickled things: avoid the former, savor the latter. (Speaking of maidens, recall if you will, a Prince the troll had known in a former life in desperate need to wed one: his ascension to the throne demanded it. The search proved more taxing than expected. Bone-white beauty and virgin territory, might as well hunt the fabled unicorn of tale and lore. Or its twin brother.) Most evenings the troll and the toad could be found at the troll's quarters, beneath the freeway overpass on Canoga Avenue, playing *Fox & Geese*, *Nine Man's Morris* or *Sailor's Two-handed Solitaire*. Wily players, they were known to skip moves, double deal, and tally scores on the four fingers and six toes of each hand and foot: the mind might wander but the body didn't lie. The toad, if one wasn't looking, would smile unassumingly and pretend that Jacks trumped Queens and Morris counted twice as much as Nine.

This one day the troll climbed up the overpass's main counterweight, hunted a piece of shade, squatted agreeably against the nearest stump of a tree and gazed out at the cars whizzing by. Passersby gaped back, in their own kind of trance or bother, and quickly forgot the lonely figure by the road they'd barely had time to register. Hours later he walked home — waddled, toddled, trundled, traipsed, troll legs being too foreshortened for much else — unpacked a jar of something mellow or ripe, flavorsome, and stared off at the distance, while the odor of pickling juice took hold of the room. Out in the front yard, he wished he could turn into stone during daylight, as in legends of old, quit his usual twisting and turning, and allow himself to forget that nothing true or real would ever come to pass. The toad, at least, had been kissed once, even if he'd been predictably

180

thrown out on his warty ass for lack of table manners.

You do know, the toad said, you make the worst of melancholics.

The troll flinched. I hate it when you do that, he said. Appearing and disappearing at will, always underfoot.

It's my nature to be underfoot, the toad countered. Under boards, stone heaps, porch steps, wood piles, dense vegetation, freshwater ponds.

One of these days, I'm going to take you up on that first part. He brandished his clawed foot at the toad.

The toad reared back. The dark spots across his spine, containing two to three warts apiece, blanched. You are in a foul mood. Something you ate?

Or possibly could. I've never pickled toad, the troll said, eyeing his friend appraisingly. Wonder how you'd keep?

The toad sniffed. Who would you cheat at backgammon with, he said.

The troll turned away, thinking: Wonder how he'd taste? Like split cod, I'll bet.

The toad took a cautionary hop back; didn't like the look on his friend's face. Let's go back to the old hoard and set up. I'll let you win this time.

Breezes, warm summer tropical air, sunshine. The toad spotted a penny stuck against a corner of the neighbor's foxtail pine. He flipped it up with one of his hind legs, spun it briefly before him and whirled it toward the troll. There you go, he said, your opening bid.

The troll examined it closely. Copper, he said. Old as the warts on your back.

I hate the way the new ones taste, like one of my great-grandmother's tits.

Watch your mouth, the troll said, pocketing the penny. I'm sure your great-grandfather never complained.

Back under the overpass they sat down at the gaming table. An antique leather-bound book, yellow-leafed, dog-eared and heavy-looking rested on one corner of the table.

What're you reading now? the toad said.

Testament of the Holy Spirit, by Cardinal Hamilcar von Sehestedt.

Never heard of it. Or him.

Few people have.

Any good?

God's life is in the Old Testament, His son's in the New, but no one ever gave a crap about the Holy Ghost. What's his story? Thousands of years of neglect. The Cardinal thought he'd give it a try. Put to paper what Joachim de Fiore only imagined.

Did he succeed?

Still on the prologue. Tiny print, lots of hemming and hawing. The Cardinal believed you had to steal up on the thing instead of knocking right at its door. Then there's the threshold question.

Yes, of course, there always is. Did he solve it?

Let's hope so, otherwise I'm wasting a lot of my time reading the damn thing.

Let's ring him up, interview him, have him answer the question before you get to page nine. Why waste another fortnight?

A bit late for a phone call or a text or snapchat. Gutted and burned at the stake at a clandestine conclave at Lyons. Unless you can read entrails and ashes, I don't think we're going to get much out of him now. Would've made for an interesting conversation, though. Seems he had shown great promise in his day, a kind of twentieth-century Thomas Aquinas. He'd surpassed all

182

the other church fathers by the time he was sixteen. Clement, Origen of Alexandria, Tertullian, Cyprian. Ancient theology, modern faith. Funny how that didn't stop the Cardinals or the Pope himself from dancing on his grave. Copies of everything he'd written burned along with him. Except for that. That made it into an undisclosed vault at the Vatican.

How'd you come by it then?

I'm a troll. Find me a warren or a den or a lair and I'll scrabble my way in and out as fast as you can flick your tongue at a fly.

Now you're pulling my leg, the toad complained.

If I did it would be to pickle it. The troll positioned the pieces on the board. Your move.

The toad studied the board. Keep talking about pickling all or parts of me and I'll find me another troll to visit with.

Who would have you? the troll snorted. In any case, the church hierarchy didn't get to every version or every copy of what the Cardinal wrote as they initially presumed. That one's been copied, translated and handed down from generation to generation, sect to sect, disciple to disciple, lost, found and lost again. I found a copy of it at an antiquarian shop on Ventura Boulevard in Sherman Oaks next to a copy of *Bell & the Dragon* and a near indecipherable *Life of Adam and Eve*. Got all three for less than a ten spot, if I remember correctly. The owner didn't know what he had. I've had all three copies for a while now but never got around to giving them much of a try. Guess the Cardinal was right — you have to steal up on a thing or it's likely not to give up much of anything.

Let's just hope it doesn't keep you up at night. Getting no response the toad decided to concentrate on the game, and moved one of his pieces forward.

My god but you're ugly, the toad said, attempting to distract the troll from guessing future moves. If I had to live with you for more than a week, I'd grow enough warts to fill a flea market.

The troll ignored him. The night dragged on. Past midnight, no one seemed to have won enough games to call it a night. They were both equally good at cheating, equally good at hiding their deceit. Easy enough because every quarter hour the rules of the game changed, a game (a variation on *Ladders & Snakes*) they had learned to play at the homeless shelter in lower Azusa where they had met, a place they'd left because everyone's shoes turned up stolen. That they didn't own any — the one because of the size of his misshapen feet; the other because shoes, no matter how well-suited, spoiled its finely timed hops — was beside the point. That they couldn't trust any of their fellow lost souls with keeping their hands off something as individual and suggestive as someone else's shoes was a matter of personal integrity neither one of them could overcome.

The troll's finger lingered over one of the pieces. Each square represented a house wherein dwelled an emotion, an emotion whose nature the player was not privy to unless the number on the thrown die and the number of moves on the board corresponded with the square upon whose house the piece landed. The object of the game was to make one's move up the ladder of emotions from least intense to most — say, for instance, glad to rapturous, having previously landed on delighted, thrilled, elated, overjoyed, jubilant, euphoric, ecstatic, and let's not forget blissful. If a player skipped an intervening emotion or forgot their order of ascendance, he (or she — to be ecumenical, in the secular, non-religious sense, of course — but no, women were never seen inside the troll's abode ... only their shadows)

184

would earn a snake, whose tail he would have to chase around the board before moving on.

Move already, the toad said.

Shhh, the troll said.

The toad sat back on his haunches and reached for a serving of Fleur du Maquis — nothing pickled for him tonight — a "promising" cheese made in Corsica from the milk of Lacaune ewes, the small wheels of which were larded with rosemary, fennel seeds, juniper berries, and the occasional bird's-eye chile.

Tell me a story, the toad said.

Shhh, I said. I know what you're trying to do.

You mean trying not to die of boredom while you contemplate your next move? Come now, something of this Cardinal you're reading.

Some believed he could keep a boat from capsizing by standing at the stern and extending his arms to the horizon.

Who'd be foolish enough to go fishing with him to figure that out?

Rabid dogs were known to meow like cats, the troll continued, after conversing with him, however casually.

Did they learn to use a litter box, too?

The troll continued to ignore him. Was provocation the first rung on a ladder leading up through annoyance to indignation? or did he have to go through discontent first? exasperation? pique? He decided it was more an act than a legitimate emotion, and made his move. No snake, the troll hooted. I have you now.

I saw that coming, said the toad. I'm just now feigning defeat.

His Eminence was a gifted child, a gifted youth and a gifted adult, gifts he took with him to his grave as he burned to a crisp

185

at the ripe old age of one hundred fifteen.

Who are we talking about?

The Cardinal, the troll said, I thought you wanted to know about the Cardinal.

I forgot, or I was trying to, the toad said, studying the game board.

Saints wept at his funeral.

Orthodox, no doubt — crybabies to a man.

We're talking about a Cardinal not a Metropolitan, you nitwit. Wrong end of the East-West religious divide.

Roman Catholic saints — even worse.

Are you going to let me tell this story or not?

Of course, of course. But how about a less contemporary tale. We both know how this one ends. What about the one with Miss Nat og Dag or the émigré Duke of Chartres or the Caliph of Beidah or Edward Butler and the streets of Greenwich?

Who's the storyteller here?

I often wonder.

Late autumn is a sight in Central Europe, the troll began, especially in Brno, the capital of what was then the Graviate of Moravia. Leaves begin to turn, a trace of snow on the horizon, the glistening waters of the Svratka, goats and sheep dreaming of the nights of winter sleep ahead.

Not sheep and goats again?

Not sheep and goats. They're secondary characters. Scenery. Décor. Staging.

But Central Europe? Central Europe for sure?

Or farther north. I'm just getting started.

He closed his eyes and thought of his mother —

Wait, wait, he? who's he? Not the Cardinal again?

Not the Cardinal. Hami, the hero of our current story.

186

What hero? What current story. You've jumped quite ahead of me somewhat. I'm a little lost here.

Ahead is where the whole thing begins, and you're supposed to be a little lost at this point. If I don't lose you now, how can I ever find you at the end of the story?

I think I'm back on the streets of Brno, with the goats and sheep.

The troll moved one of his pieces and began again. Hami closed his eyes and thought about his mother and the stories she told of the old country, a place not so ancient or faraway she could not reach back through memory and touch its heart. She would speak of the Spirits of Bath and Barn, who were easily appeased by the placing of a robin's egg in the right place — the trick, of course, was to find the right place. Of the Spirit of Joy, whose name escaped her, spruce and fair, of his moon-white horse and boyish bare feet. The Spirit would ride the countryside, hair unbound, laughing at earth and sky.

"Where he set his foot,
The corn grows in mountains;
Wherever he glances,
Every spring he sees fountains ... "

Ah, Hami, his mother would tell him, don't forget what it's like to be young and free and full of wonder. The past, the present, too, for that matter, will eat the future if you let it. Do you remember Sœlingsdlstúnga, Hami? It's mostly a legend, I know, but you do remember, don't you? Yes, mother, he said, dipping a hand in the river. That was not quite true. Sœlingsdlstúnga was neither legend nor memory to him. He liked the sliding slipping suggestion of that ancient word; it promised a brief

187

April and May, a longer summer; and he didn't like disappointing his mother. Remember the old farm there, his mother said, the old farmer. His two sons, she went on, Arnór and Sveinn.

They come in pairs, don't they? Cain and Abel. Twiddle Dee and Twiddle Dum, Simon and Garfunkel, mac and cheese.

You keep interrupting, I'll never get finished here.

If I don't interrupt, you'll never get started.

The troll continued, as if he were the only one of the two in the room. They're both dead now, the mother said. The father, too. The entire village. What a tragedy.

Hold on there, hold on. You just got to the end of the story before I did.

What are you babbling about?

Everyone's dead, you silly old troll. If that doesn't spell the end of a story, I don't know what else does.

There was a little girl. Ellsá Hannsson. Before you ask, before you interrupt again, no one knew who the father was, had been, remember the entire village perished. It could have been either one of the two brothers.

The entire village?

The entire village.

One of us needs a lesson on the meaning of words, how language works.

The village, the troll went on, was situated between two massive hillsides. The village elders built one of two churches below one of the outcrops, the steeple practically kissing its central ledge. But not nearly so. Some in the village speculated it had something to do with unrequited love. But never mind all that. What you need to remember is that she was an exceptional beauty by the age of nineteen. She was also extraordinarily tall. Only when standing, however. When she sat down,

188

which was more often than not, more often than she should have, good-bye tallness. The villagers nicknamed her 'Sister Longlegs'. A cruel name but a telling gesture. I don't think anyone knows anything about anything, Longlegs told her friend Marit. A Tuesday, I think. They were having dinner or cooking breakfast; things could get rather complicated rather quickly with these two; it made them inseparable. Especially the fell-maker, Longlegs continued. He got good old jaunty Gubjør with child, which turned out to be a changeling, right around its third birthday. A naughty child and a naughty changeling, especially after the charm she used to get him to speak proper Finnish. If he hadn't been a brat before, he was one now.

Finnish? I thought we were in Iceland. Sœlingsdlstúnga is definitely Icelandic.

Finland? Iceland? Places tend to bleed into each other when you're in that part of the world.

You'd have to cross an unmitigated ocean, the North Atlantic, I believe, back and forth, perhaps twice, perhaps never, to get Finland and Iceland to be in the same part of the world. Never mind the Baltic.

Snow, freezing weather, more snow, same part of the world.

It's your story. Who am I to want for details.

The troll harrumphed and went back to his tale. As you know Marit, Longlegs said. It was nearly lunchtime. Her mother's lunchtime, as a matter of fact. The dear old thing would have to wait. As you know Marit, Gubjør would have none of it. Her child was not a changeling, she would insist, rather loudly, rather obnoxiously, he's just precocious. 'Any variable is a term. Any constant symbol from the signature is a term. Therefore, an expression of the form $f(t_1,...,t_n)$, where f is an n-ary function symbol, and $t_1,...,t_n$ are terms, is again a term,' he would go around saying, as though he were asking for no more than a second glass of milk. That didn't take away from the fact that his nose looked like a cat's, an ugly cat, mangy, sclerotic, hunchbacked, and that he had an extra hand growing out of the middle of his back. He would wave it at you teasingly, relentlessly, as you approached him and his siblings and his nanny on Strömhugget Platz (his other limbs being otherwise quite helpless). No one ever waved back. It would lead to long somber afternoons at the Gubjør manse, especially during high summer, when the Platz would be teeming with townspeople in for the farmer's market, you'd expect people to be friendlier, more responsive. Jenny was never the same after that one wave on Sunday. Went home to a husband who kept asking for kippers, bacon, spinach, new potato salad, none of them in season. They went to bed early. The husband was a light sleeper and slept next to the wall. He couldn't very well look out to the streetlight through any kind of window, there were none, there was just the wall, and pretend he was a moth and that the warmth was comforting and that soon enough the seasons would turn and he'd have his kippers in hand. He was awake past midnight. And suddenly the room glowed red, as though someone had stirred the fire. And sure enough, there he was next to the fire, stirring and stirring and stirring, a man uglier than anything he could ever describe. 'The nose, Jenny,' he told his wife later that morning, 'the nose was bent in three places, one eye, the middle one I think, staring stark-right at the bridge of its nose, the other at its brow line. Its skin looked mottled. A jagged varicolored tooth balanced itself just this side of the curve of its upper lip as though it was deliberately trying to jump back into its mouth but it was out of practice.' That night Jenny's husband could hardly speak as he watched the dreadful little misshapen thing stir his fire like it

190

was trundle soup and the spices had to be kept from separating by the troubling of the ladle. There was a sound from the other side of the wall just then, like someone scratching to be let in, and a voice insinuated itself through the joists. 'Lars, me darling, have ye got 'im yet?'

Wait, wait, we're in Finland, aren't we?

Yes, yes, we've established that.

And you have him talking like an Irishman?

What are you talking about? It's the disagreeable bloke's second wife doing the talking, and that's how they all sound in Finland, especially in the nineteenth century, and especially in that particular fishing village, cut off from the mainland. It's the translation you're complaining about.

I'm complaining about something.

'Lars, me darling, have ye got 'im yet?' the voice said.

'Eye, Roberta, I think someone's told ye a lie.'

'What'd'ya mean me darling?'

'There's no wee child here, me love. There's no child tat tall.'

'"Turn right and turn right again," Skalunda said. It's got to be the right house.'

'No Roberta, ye got it wrong, me old girl. "Turn right and turn right again on Skalunda Street," that's what he said.'

'Oh my, oh my,' the voice said. 'Let's get a'moving, then. I'm awfully rattled by me hunger, and we've got morning to find Skalunda Street, never mind right and right and turn and turn.'

Just as suddenly Lars was gone and so was the fire. It had to have been a coincidence, Marit said. I agree, Longlegs said, but why just then and who could have planned it? The Fillmores no longer live there, so we can't ask them. Do you think we'll ever hear from them? No, Marit said, what a shame, the entire village. A wee child Marit, Longlegs said, a wee child. The world's drowning in babies and here two strangers turning and turning to steal one of their own. And poor Jenny's husband in love with a wall and Gjertud Kostibakken crying and crying and crying as though she could buy back her tears at the end of creation and her boy with the wasting sickness and the water spell and the goblin spell and the corpse spell and no one's seemed to have noticed they don't work on a boy, not if he's teething, might as well count on Satan to plead your case to the heavens and the mill stream dry as lions in winter and nowhere to bathe all those crying babies and the church's no good, Presbyterians and Quakers, 'that's holy water,' the priest says, 'good only for sinners and starvelings,' as though babies are exempt from sinning, as though anyone's seen a starveling in many a century, as though Skalunda Street wasn't named after Skalunda, as though one couldn't conjure for sickness and conjure for pain, conjure it off and call it again, as though Marit's husband wasn't gunning for her for spending so much time gossiping with Longlegs, as though Gubjør didn't dream of a normal child, Jenny's husband of Jenny's brother Bedelund, Arnór and Sveinn of that vacation in Guam that was never taken, Hami of a robin's egg on Sunday, the Cardinal of a second edition of his magnum opus, Miss Nat og Dag of her own story, if only two chapters, the Duke of Chartres of a return to his country, the Caliph of Beidah of that one magic carpet, Edward Butler of people remembering his three-wheeled petrol vehicle, Greenwich of people thinking that it's time was anything but mean, Longlegs of Marit's cheating husband, as though Lars hadn't gone into the room for the warmth instead of a miserable baby, as though —

Hah! I won, I won, I won! The toad jumped off his stool and hopped around as though his feet were on fire.

Sure enough, he had the snake. It was not chasing its tail.

I knew it, the troll said. You had me talking to the air so I'd forget what a conniving little toad you are.

Your fault you fell in love with the sound of your voice and trying to mesmerize me out of watching your every scheming move with a bunch of senseless characters with not enough substance to roll into a cigar.

Get out, get out of my house before I step on you, the troll bellowed. In Calabasas parents and children had a run of bad dreams for a month without quite knowing why.

Troll, troll, has his father's mismatched toes.

The troll threw the wheel of cheese at him. The toad ducked, twisted in the direction of the runaway prize, flicked its tongue at it as though to spear a trout. Catching it on his second try, he bounded toward the door.

Troll, troll, has his mother's undiagnosed woes.

The troll stood there, as though he had turned to stone. I will pickle you, I swear, he shouted, warts and all.

His eyes felt muddy and swollen, as though he were about to cry. He blinked away at nothing and took a deep breath. What did he have to cry about anyway? He remembered the found penny. It was still in his pocket — that stupid, old toad wasn't the only one who knew how to cheat. He sat down on his heels. He was out of cheese and for the moment had lost his love for anything pickled. He was hungry and miserable and hungry and miserable and hungry. He would have to go out hunting. A toothsome virgin would do. This was the San Fernando Valley, however, it could take weeks, years. He bent over, nose to the ground. Perhaps the old toad had missed a cheese crumb or two in his hurry to escape.

The Haircut

The house had small rectangular windows on either side of the front door. They didn't let in much light, but ours was the only house in the neighborhood with windows like these, someone's architectural fancy, and I loved them. They were each a different color like snow cones. I remember running home at the close of the school day, regretting the end of my first grade adventures, missing the friends I was making, but glad to be home at last. I would stop to run my tongue across the colors — blue, red, green, yellow — as though I could somehow taste the house.

For four weeks one of the windows was broken. For four weeks it was bandaged over with a piece of cardboard. For four weeks I didn't go to school. Four weeks of my father following my mother around the house, room to room, trying to get her to talk to him. Four weeks of having my mouth bandaged over with mercurochrome. Four weeks of scabs that wouldn't heal. I can still taste the mercurochrome, and remember, too, licking my lips over and over again, hoping this would somehow help them heal.

That's why I hate haircuts. The smell of hair tonic, the buzz of clippers, the stare of a mirror you can't seem to escape, all bring back to me those four weeks, my smashed window.

"I don't need a haircut."

"Sure you do, honey. I can't have you running around looking like an orphan, now can I?"

"I want to look like an orphan. I don't want a haircut!"

"Go on, go along with Daddy. He's getting a haircut, too. Learn to be a man, just like him."

I didn't know what she meant. My father was not one to give lessons. My every act or deed would get from him nothing more than a stare. He wouldn't say anything, wouldn't yell or shout, wouldn't encourage or correct, he would just stare.

"I don't want to go. I won't go."

"Come on," my father said. He yanked me out the door.

The street we lived on was only half a street. At its dead end was a small park dotted with trees, picnic tables grouped around them to take advantage of their long and cooling shade. At any given time, a number of men, older and retired, some unemployed, clustered around the tables, loudly playing dominoes. That day, as usual, my grandfather and his friends had claimed a table near the swimming pool at one corner of the park. Kids could be heard thrashing about in the pool, their threats and accusations ringing in the air. The old men's curses, no less childish in threat and accusation, would hold the air at times as though in response. Suddenly, out of nowhere, a single bark of laughter was heard. The kids and the old men joined it in echo.

My father waved at my grandfather as we passed by and yelled out, "Haircut." My grandfather waved at me, and I yelled out, "Me too," as my father hurried me along.

From time to time friends of mine have complained that I walk too fast to enjoy anything like a view. But I learned to walk at my father's side. A short man, he walked faster than men twice his height. I was afraid he'd turn the corner before me; he'd leave me stranded somewhere, and I'd really be an orphan.

My father and Frank the barber had been war buddies during the Korean War. I didn't know what that meant at the time — it was something special. The two or three men who hung around the barbershop (forever in need of a haircut, I believed), Frank and my father were constantly trading war stories, indicting each other's telling of their experience in war: ship time, landing, hand-to-hand combat, claiming some deed no one, not any one of them, could have ever pulled off. All in a language hard to understand, part of the clip of scissors, the rasp of razor edging up over the back of my neck. Certain words would bend them over in tight gusts of laughter. Leaning over the sink behind him, Frank the barber would wipe away at the tears on his face, take a deep breath and between gasps say to no one in particular, "Oh, God!" I didn't understand what was being said or the why of the laughter but I wanted to join in.

We spent an hour at Frank's barbershop. He kept stopping, telling jokes between sneezes of laughter, his razor taking bites out of the air instead of an ear.

We stopped off at my grandfather's table on our way home.

"You almost look human, young man," my grandfather said.

"I don't want to look human. I want to look like a little boy."

"They're human, too, you know."

"But only sometimes," someone said.

Everyone at the table laughed and turned toward me. I did that, I thought, and wondered if making people laugh was a way of being grown up.

"What did Frank have to say for himself?" my grandfather asked.

"Not much," my father answered. "Stuff about the war."

"That man never gets enough of that war," my grandfather said. "You'd think he'd fought it single-handed."

"He got a tattoo in the war — a big cat with red eyes."

My father stared at me, and I was a little boy again. But I'd show him.

"He said my father didn't get a tattoo 'cause he was scared —"

Everyone turned toward me. Grins appeared on some of the faces. I wouldn't look at my father, but imagined his stare melting into a smile.

"He said he was scared 'cause he was a faggot, nothing but a big cocksucker —"

I had expected great roars of laughter, tidal and magic. Instead, I heard a sharp intake of breath, and a cough like teeth being spit out of a bloody mouth.

"Damn you!" my father threw out at me. He tried to start up from the table, violently grabbing for me across it, and stumbled. I jumped up and ran. Frank's cackled shrieks had split the air like a hyena's when he'd said it. My father and his friends had joined in out of sheer outrage. I had understood only the laughter.

I ran and ran. I couldn't seem to get nearer my destination. And I needed a destination. I would be able stop, and everything would be all right. I could hear my father behind me.

"You bastard, you little bastard!"

I turned into an alley... — but I was up in the air, my father shaking me by the shoulders, "You little bastard!"

"What's all the commotion — I could hear you down the street." My mother had come out onto the porch. I squealed and reached for her, but my father pulled me away. My mother poked questions at him.

198

He had a shoe in his hand. He held me against the railing and smashed it across my mouth. My mother screamed, "Dennis, Dennis, stop — "

My mother caught my father's hand as it swung toward me for perhaps the third or fourth or fifth time. (Once, it was only once.) The shoe fell out of his hand and, as he reached for it, she hurled it away. The shoe crashed through the window.

"Damn you," my mother screamed at my father. "Look what you made me do!" She grabbed me by my elbow and rushed me inside the house. I turned around and looked at my father's hand, as though he was still holding the shoe.

That's when my mother stopped talking to my father. For four weeks. After a while, she spoke to him again. After a while, my mouth healed, and I was allowed to go back to school. After a while, the window was replaced with a shiny new one. I would run home from school, go to my windows and lick each one in turn. Each one but the new one. It had not come with the house and it didn't belong. I would touch my finger to my tongue and play it across the new window — quickly, like a burn.

Acknowledgements

The autopsy in "A Noontime Brightness Will Shine for Thee" was freely cobbled together from several online samples of criminal autopsies. The poems in "Lorca at Five O'clock in the Afternoon" are from Lorca's *Poets in New York: A Bilingual Edition* and *The Selected Poems of Federico Garcia Lorca*. The rock and roll songs quoted throughout the collection speak for themselves, their time, and mine. Then there's Blake's "Infant Sorrow," "Are you lonesome tonight?" by way of Elvis Presley, Euclid's *Elements*, Book 1, Proposition 27, "The Witch" and "Túngustapi" from *Scandinavian Folk & Fairy Tales*, Lowell, Kubler, Lawrence, Bessie Smith, Hemingway (in name only), Webster's *Third New International Dictionary*, Baum, samplings, cuttings, half-quotes, echoes, bad habits entirely my own.

Dana Gorbea-Leon was born in Ponce, Puerto Rico. He came to Los Angeles, California, when he was seven years old. He's had nine lives, one in state government, one as a union organizer, one as a community activist, another as a newspaper writer and columnist, another in the advertising field. Currently he works in marketing in the healthcare industry. No pets, no children, no alibis. He's tackling a science-fiction novel and a memoir. Currently resides in Alhambra, California.